i

c

o

p

e

CCM Design by Michael J. Seidlinger
Cover and Interior Design by Ryan W. Bradley
Cover photograph by Chmee2/Valtameri and used under a
CC Attribution 3.0 Unported License
Antler illustration by Alan R. Engstrom

ISBN: 978-1-937865-53-5

For more information, find CCM at:

copingmechanisms.net

NOTHING BUT THE DEAD AND DYING

STORIES BY RYAN W. BRADLEY

For all the workers on the North Slope,
especially the mud doggers.

And for Lisa, always.

STORIES

"This ain't going to be no goddamn Sunday school picnic."

—Kent Haruf, Plainsong

HAUL ROAD

Even at twenty-five miles an hour the snowfall looks like a TV left on through dawn. French is on the radio, letting the checkpoint know how fucked the storm is. There's nothing we can do to not end up in a ditch but try to watch what we can see of the road, or worse, the pipeline. Of course, the checkpoint's still timing us, that's the rules and breaking the haul road's speed limit is the kind of thing that'll get you shit-canned.

French hangs the mic on the dash. "Hey, G.P.," he says, picking up where he left off, "how's a Green Peace turd like yourself do with the ladies?"

I fold the map across my legs. Doing twenty-five we're still looking at forty minutes.

"You daydreaming about all that twat?"

"Being a democrat isn't the same as being in Green Peace," I say. "Anyway, what were you guys doing in my wallet?"

"Calm down, Junior. We've got to be careful, in case we got a certified Commie on our crew." French grins big, showing a few holes in his smile. "You're paying enough attention to that clock for the both of us." He taps the green numbers blinking on the radio. "How long you figure?"

"Forty minutes."

"Jesus."

"Could be worse."

"Really?" French turns to me. "So this isn't the first time you've driven the haul road, huh?"

"It is," I say, though French knows as much.

He flings his hand at the windshield, his nails clanking against the glass. "This shit gets people killed."

"What kind of rookies break a fucking drill?"

"Happens to the best of them. Your day will come."

"Bullshit," I say, and French shakes his head.

"Come on, it's a long drive. Tell me about all that fresh-out-of-high-school ass you're getting."

"I've got a girlfriend."

"No joke?"

"Name's Sara."

"Settling down at twenty-two? You really are wet behind the ears. So, how's that going?"

The wipers blur back and forth across the windshield, without a chance of keeping up.

"What'd they do to their drill anyway?"

"Hit too much rebar, I guess. Don't matter," French says, jerking his thumb at the backseat, "we've still got to take them this one. So, she a hot little thing, your girl?"

"Fuck."

"Nevermind. Shit."

"I just don't want to think about it."

"Problems in paradise? Lay it on me, I've lost more women than you've met."

"It's all fucked," I say, tapping my fingers on my knee, a nervous habit that drives Sara nuts.

French is hunched over the steering wheel trying to find the road.

"What could be fucked about twenty-two-year-old pussy?"

"Sara's pregnant."

He doesn't take his eyes off the road, but it feels like he's staring directly at me. "Shit, you got yourself in deep, didn't you?"

"Believe me, I know."

"You don't know a damn thing."

The snow is making me dizzy and I'm glad French is driving.

"Well, you two talked about it or what? How you leaning?"

"Like the Tower of Pisa."

French laughs. "Yeah?" He sits back long enough to shift around a bit before hunching forward again. "When did you find out?"

"Couple weeks ago." My last R&R, two weeks at home, sleeping with Sara, getting drunk at whatever bar we stumbled into, until one night she wanted to stay in. Watch a movie. "She went to a doctor the day before I flew back to Deadhorse." I shove my hands between my thighs.

"Crap way to leave things."

"Definitely."

"What's she think about it all?"

I fix my eyes on the dashboard. "She's Irish Catholic, she wouldn't ever... you know." I still can't believe she didn't slap me just for saying the word.

The radio crackles. "You numb-nuts out there or what? Truck Two-O-Five did you read?"

French picks up. "You going to keep us warm?"

"We weren't getting a response for over five minutes. What's going on?"

"We didn't hear shit from you until now," French says.

"That's not good. You guys need to be checking in like clockwork. How's the road?"

"The road? Fuck off." French slams the receiver back on its dock. "Assholes sitting there at a damn desk. You never want to be one of those guys, G.P., never." He looks at me and I nod. "Those guys with desk jobs, they've forgotten what real work is."

For a second I picture French as my father, that we're driving to Fairbanks or something. Going camping, "Just a boys' weekend," he'd tell my mother. I look at French. I don't know, but I imagine wherever my dad is he's got a full set of teeth.

"I don't think I can do it," I say.

French taps the brakes and we start to fishtail, then skid back on track. He looks at me, his eyes ball bearings, his jaw tight.

"What? You little prick, you're thinking of bailing? Listen, I've got two little girls. Been to jail twice. Compared to anything else this is the sweet life."

"Sure," I say.

He waves his arms at the blizzard. "This, right here, is a goddamn piece of paradise."

"That why everybody talks about saving up for houses in Hawaii or Florida? It's like the goddamn Alaskan state mantra."

He digs into his jeans pocket and pulls out a small metal poker chip. "You know what this is?" he asks, holding it in front of my face.

I shake my head.

"Five years sober. My first meeting was the day my wife told me she was pregnant."

"I'm not a drunk."

"Never said you were."

The only sound is the heater on full blast, and I strain, wondering if I can hear the snow falling.

"Kids happen, G.P.," French says, his voice quieter than before. "People do their best, it's all they can. Your only choice is whether you're going to raise that kid, or puss out."

"I'd be a horrible father," I say.

"Jesus. You can't get a much worse candidate for fatherhood than me, but I got my shit together. I work in this damn Popsicle stand six out of every eight weeks so my wife can be home to take care of our girls."

"I don't know the first thing about being a dad. I'm only twenty-two, you said it yourself."

"I'll say something else, too," French says. "You don't have much choice." He lifts his hat and rubs his forehead.

"There are a lot of choices."

"Name one." French eases on the gas, but doesn't stop. The snow swirls around us. "Got one yet?"

I shake my head. We should be at the checkpoint in less than twenty minutes.

"Two-O-Five, you there?"

French doesn't pick up. He takes his eyes off the road to look at me again.

"Well," I say.

"Truck Two-O-Five. Two-O-Five."

French squeezes the radio with his ash gray fingers. "We're here," he says. "Maybe twenty minutes out."

"Why don't you do the checking in next time? Say ten minutes?"

"Sure thing."

We drive in silence and I strain to see the road. The brim of French's Carhartt hat is touching the windshield. With the heater on, the cab is thick with sweat. The tires slip, slight at first, then the bed of the truck is sideways. We're spinning. I brace one hand on the seat and hold onto the handle above the door with the other.

"Mother-bitch, shit-ass," French says, but it's distant, like I'm a kid eavesdropping from the backseat.

We go off the road with a bump that sends my head into the roof, even with my seatbelt on. French is still pumping on the gas, trying to get us back on track, but we're shit out of luck, and he knows it. The truck lurches as he lets off the pedal and we spit backward into the nothingness beyond the road. Sliding, we tip on our side. My body snaps forward, my hat falling off as I slam into the dashboard. There's a short burst from the horn, French thrown into the wheel. Even though I don't see anything out my window, I know I'm looking at the ground.

French is hanging over me, suspended by his seatbelt. The cab's light is dim and flickering, but I can see his forehead's starting to swell.

"Jesus fuck," he says. "You all right, G.P.?"

I take a deep breath. "Yeah." I can feel the lump growing on my own head, and the burn across my chest from the belt doing its best to hold me still.

"You know what stopped us don't you?"

I nod, but he says it anyway.

"The pipeline."

"How are we going to get out?"

"The only way we can," he says. "My window." He reaches for the crank on the side of his door, rolls the window down. The musty cab chills instantly. "Better pull on your coat."

French shows his missing teeth. I reach below the seat, where I had stuffed my extra gear.

"I'm going to pull myself out, then you can pass me mine."

French grabs the window frame with one hand and undoes his seatbelt with the other. His legs drop in front of my face. I smell the dried mud on the bottom of his Xtra Tuffs. He grunts and pulls himself halfway out of the window.

"Couldn't see a tit out here if it was in your face," he says. "Hand me my shit before I freeze to death."

I unbuckle myself and grab his jacket, wadded up in the backseat. The concrete drill is in two pieces on the floor of the cab. I plant my feet on the door and stand up, reaching French's jacket out the window.

"I think I should take a look around. See if the radio's working."

I hunch down and grab the mic, my hand already so cold it's hard to grip. I hold down the button and am greeted by fuzz.

"This is truck Two-O-Five," I say. "Do you read?" More fuzz. I try again with the same result. "I think it's busted."

"Shit." I hear French push off the frame of the truck. "Snow's over my knees," he says. "Can you get out?"

I zip up my coat, pull on my gloves, and replace my baseball hat with a knit one that I pull over my ears. Reaching both hands out the window, I pull myself up and into the white.

"Drill's broke, too," I say, adjusting so I'm sitting on the door.

"We got enough to worry about. Get down here." French is barely visible until I slide off the truck and land next to him. "We've got to check out the damage around back," he says. "We'll go around the bed until we find the pipeline."

We walk with our hands out, holding onto the truck. I can hear French's breathing ahead of me. He stops and I push between him and the truck. I reach out with my free hand, waiting to touch something solid. When I do, the snow around my legs is stained black and I lean forward. There's a faint glow from the tail lights, and I see the glinting rush.

French taps me on the shoulder, mumbling more cusses. "We can't stay here."

My glove is wet with oil, the familiar smell throws me back to my dad working on his truck in the driveway.

"What choice do we have?"

"The checkpoint can't be far. We've got to find the road." French slaps me on the back and turns around.

I turn my back to the growing pool of black snow and fight through the drift. At the front of the truck, French says if we follow the headlights we'll find the road.

"If the bed's in the pipeline," he says, "the truck must be facing that way." He takes his hand off the hood and pushes on. "Stay close."

"Right behind you," I say, sticking out a hand to touch his back.

The ground slopes upward and I feel gravel under my boots. The snow on the road is only shin high, but my legs feel like I've been running in sand.

"Should I have brought the drill?" I ask, frost budding on my lips.

"Busting the pipeline open, no one's going to be worrying about a drill." French's breathing is growing heavier.

I pull the collar of my coat over my face, yank my hat down tighter. The first day of training they said to report spills of any liquid immediately. I never thought it would be more than a joke to use when someone was dumping the remains of a cup of coffee. But behind us product is spilling at a rate that causes heart attacks for environmentalists and oil tycoons both.

"How far do you think?"

"Not far, G.P." French says.

I can feel his breath heating my cheeks.

"Got to keep warm." He is by my side, putting an arm around my shoulder. He pulls me close, the way a father might.

People get lost in weather like this, everything looking the same, and for a moment I think it wouldn't be so bad to disappear into the tundra. But French wrapping himself around me has got me thinking I would know when a kid needed comfort.

French coughs, spurts of frozen breath cracking the air. "Fatherhood's not looking so bad now, is it?"

Though the cold is painful in my lungs, I laugh.

The wind picks up, whips through my jacket and hat, exposing the cracks, tearing at my skin. I focus on feeling the road underfoot, tell myself we're still on gravel. In front of us is a blank canvas, an empty field of white. I stare ahead against the wind and snow, begging my eyes to be tricked into seeing the yellow light of a lantern, showing the way.

ALL THAT HE KNEW

Frank stood from the bed, which was really just an old mattress on the floor. Peggy was still sleeping, strands of her hair sticking out from under a mound of blankets and old sweaters. While a pot of coffee brewed, he used a butter knife to scrape ice off the inside of the living room window. Frank had notified the super every day for a month and still nothing had been done about the poor seal on the windows or the broken heater. Their apartment was on the bottom corner of the building so heat didn't trap well to begin with.

Frank poured a cup of coffee and took it to the bathroom, which quickly filled with steam from the shower. For a few minutes he was naked and warm. He pulled his work jeans on over long underwear, finished the coffee in his cup, and sat on the toilet to put on his socks. There was a hole in the heel of one, and in the toe of the other. All their socks had holes, his and Peggy's. They wore second pairs over the first, hoping the holes wouldn't align.

He kneeled by the side of the mattress and lifted the blankets to kiss Peggy. Her eyelids flickered.

"Brr," she said.

"Sorry. I left you some coffee," Frank said, and re-buried her head. She wasn't supposed to have caffeine, or at least the baby wasn't. But she'd have something warm to think about. On the way out he grabbed a can of baked beans from the kitchen cupboard. There was a hot plate in the office, but he liked heating the cans with a welder's torch.

The super didn't salt the parking lot on Saturday mornings, so Frank walked with slow, exaggerated steps, like an elderly person who'd lost his walker. He put the can of beans in the cup holder and started his car, blasting the defrost. He did his best to scrape ice from the windshield, creating a porthole to look out until the car warmed up. The brakes squealed with condensation and the muffler backfired as he pulled out of the apartment complex.

There was only one other car in the lot at work, his boss's Suburban. The mechanics usually clocked in by six, that should have been his first clue. Frank's boss, Jerry was sitting at his desk, still in his Carhartt jacket.

"What's the action, boss?"

Frank set the can of beans on the counter and dumped leftover sludge from the coffee pot.

"Have a seat," Jerry said.

The coils of the space heater behind Jerry's desk glowed a dull orange. The metal casing expanded with the heat, ticking and groaning. The smell of burnt dust filled the small room.

"I'm afraid we're letting you go," Jerry said.

Even on a day where the temperature wasn't bound to get above zero, Frank broke out in a sweat.

"Why?"

"I like you Frank, you're just not the right fit for us." Jerry stood and swiped an envelope off his desk. "I told Sheila to cut the check to carry you through the month."

It was the 28th.

"Good luck, Frank," Jerry said, extending his small, smooth hand.

The windshield had defrosted enough to run the wipers. They pushed melted ice back and forth. Frank leaned his head against the window. The glass was still plenty cold. If he were to cry, Frank thought, his face might actually freeze to the window.

He took out his cell phone to call Peggy, but hung up before it could ring. This was already his third job in the last year and they had an ultrasound coming up. His own father had left as soon as he found out he was going to have a kid. Frank looked him up when he turned 18, found out he was doing time at Goose Creek. That was all Frank needed to know.

Frank opened the glove compartment. He pulled out the Taurus .357 his mother had given him when he started snowshoeing on his own in high school, in case he came upon a bear. The rubber grip was cracked. Frank had only ever used it to shoot at cans and bottles. There were two bullets in the cylinder.

He spun the cylinder and pointed the gun at the windshield, pulled the trigger. The hammer snapped. Nothing. He cut the wipers and reversed out of his parking spot.

The bank was in a strip mall. Most of the other businesses around it were shut down. Frank opened the envelope Jerry had given him and looked at the check. He shoved it in his pocket and got out of the car. He looked around the empty parking lot and stuck the Taurus in the waist of his jeans, making sure it was covered by his coat.

There was only one teller and no one waiting. Frank put his check on the counter.

"Just a deposit," he said.

Frank looked around. There were two security cameras. The teller went about running the check and clacking away on his keyboard.

Right now the baby was probably kicking at Peggy's belly. She said it was most active when she ate breakfast. Frank hadn't felt it move yet. Not once. He was always at work by the time Peggy was eating.

The gun slipped and Frank did his best to adjust it without looking suspicious. His heart was pounding so hard he was sure the teller could hear it. And wasn't the deposit taking longer than normal?

But then the man was sliding a receipt across the counter and telling Frank to have a good day. Frank gave a small grunt, and kept his eyes down. He clutched the receipt, the ink smudging in his sweaty palm as he walked back to his car.

The apartment parking lot was still iced over and unsalted. It was starting to snow. Frank tried to walk slowly, but the closer he got to the apartment the more his pace picked up. He slipped with nearly every step, but kept his feet moving. He burst in the front door and didn't bother removing his boots, tracking mud across the carpet from the door to the kitchen.

Peggy was standing by the stove, her hands peeking out from the sleeves of one of Frank's sweaters and suspended above a pot of boiling water. Steam laced between her fingers.

"What are you doing?" she said.

Frank shoved his hand into his coat and pulled out a package of baby socks.

"Got these," he said.

"What about work?"

Frank shook his head. Peggy's face blanched and her smile melted.

"Oh," she said.

Frank dropped to his knees, rested his head against the globe of her belly. He slid his hand under her shirt and she braced at his cold touch. He held his hand there, against her, and waited to feel the flutter of a new life.

THE LONG GRASS

Julius jumped from one hay roll to another and another. Two and a half feet between each, they stretched across the entire field. He didn't want to think about his dad's dead dog, Cash. He paused, took a breath, jumped.

"J-Bird," Amy shouted.

Julius grinned and stopped to let her catch up. Perched on top of the roll he could barely see the road. He wanted it completely out of sight. Amy landed next to him.

"Why are you going so fast? Don't you want to wait for me?" she asked.

"Don't you want to be faster?"

Julius launched to the next roll. His shoulder ached every time he landed. He looked at the compass he kept in his pocket. His father had given it to him for his seventh birthday, the same day his parents' divorce became official. Julius carried it with him every day. Amy hopped down and, turning, he saw her sprint toward the line of trees that framed the hayfield to the West.

"C'mon J." Her golden hair flopped across her face as she turned her head in the direction of the river.

Julius waved her away, his attention on the next stop along his route. Playing it cool was the only way he'd get close to a girl. He knew that much from watching the other boys at school. Julius was ashamed to be fourteen and not have seen a breast yet, or felt a girl's tongue in his mouth. He'd been trying to kiss her, touch her, since they had first met a few weeks back when he arrived from Oregon to spend the summer with his father.

Julius swung his arms, and his feet lifted simultaneously. He didn't watch the ground, but kept his eyes on the curve of the roll in front of him, spotting his landing point.

As long as he kept the line of trees to his immediate right he couldn't get lost. Scanning the field for Amy, he saw she was by the riverbank. She waved her arms wildly. Julius leapt. Hands on knees he looked back toward the river, Amy was hopping up and down now. She must have found something, he thought, knowing what it was, but hoping he was wrong.

Julius fell on the last roll and his shoulder throbbed, but he'd made it, although when he looked right the trees were no longer there. A border of dirt, about as wide as Julius was tall, separated the hayfield from a field of corn. The day after Julius arrived for the summer, his dad and he had walked the fields with Cash and his dad warned him about playing in the corn. He'd stood there in front of the first row of stalks, six foot four, over half a foot taller than Julius, arms crossed, and said in fields that hadn't been harvested it was easier to get lost than Julius could imagine.

"Especially when you're no taller than the corn itself," he'd added.

Julius had focused on his dad's leathery arms and shrugged. Cash took off along the dirt border, but Julius' father shouted, "heel" and the dog returned. The two of them walked on, while Julius stared into the corn, imagining what might be on the other side.

"Thinking about getting yourself lost, J-Bird?" Amy said, suddenly at his side.

"Something like that." Julius swallowed hard and forced a chuckle.

"That's my dad's corn, five acres of it, anyway. There's a road on the other side and more corn on the other side of that."

Julius nodded, ran his fingers along the sides of the compass in his pocket.

"Why didn't you come when I waved you over?" she asked.

"Didn't see you."

Amy grabbed his hand and pulled him away from the corn. He watched her butt in her jean shorts. Her tan calves glistened with sweat. She was muscular, her biceps something he'd never seen on a girl. In fact, she wasn't much like any girl he'd ever known. She liked football, she said, and could pack away as much food as Julius.

"There's something you've got to see," she said. "It's gross."

Julius winced, knowing there was no way out. Amy showed him every worm, every insect, every dead mouse she found when they were in the fields. She pulled him forward, making his bruised shoulder burn.

The dog's black and white fur was damp and matted with blood. Amy pulled a branch from a nearby tree and shoved it under its stiff body, flipping the corpse over on the riverbank. Tufts of fur were scattered in the grass, and the dog's skin looked like it had been shredded. It was Cash. Julius shook, holding back a rush of bile rising in his throat.

"That's your dad's dog, isn't it?" Amy asked, poking Cash's collar with the stick.

Julius turned away. Every time he closed his eyes he saw himself dragging Cash's body to the river, dumping it in and willing it far away. But it had washed up on the other side of the road.

"Yeah, that's Cash. I'll tell my dad when he gets home," Julius said.

He had no intention of telling his father about the dog. Julius' father had gotten Cash in the divorce, the only thing he'd really fought for, giving up the custody battle as soon as Julius' mother dangled the rights to the dog. But it would be the fact that Julius snuck one of his dad's guns, shot it on his own, that would earn him the belt.

"It looks like he was shot," Amy said.

Julius grabbed a handful of pebbles and tossed them into the river. He nodded and shrugged and Amy kept commenting on how disgusting Cash looked, increasing Julius' nausea.

"Who would shoot a dog?"

"I don't know," Julius said, turning his head.

"I guess we can just leave him here." Amy poked the ground with her stick.

Julius shuffled away from the river, hoping Amy would follow. When she did he was relieved. He reached for her hand and held it tightly.

They walked back toward the middle of the field and the hay rolls. Amy's hand was sweaty in his, and his heart raced looking at her breasts. He pulled her in front of him, put her back to a hay roll, kissed her. The first time he tried to kiss her, a few days before, she had giggled as soon as his lips met hers, but this time he felt her give in to his touch.

His hands moved with a fury over Amy's butt, and up her waist until his hands were on her chest. Amy turned her head.

"What?" Julius asked.

Amy pushed his chest gently, backing him away, and ran off toward the river. Always the damn river, Julius thought. When he caught up, she was sitting on a large rock in the middle of the water. Her shoes were on the bank, socks folded and tucked into their respective sneaker. Julius kicked off his own shoes, nearly putting one in the river, and walked toward her. The water was cold.

"What did you do this morning before I called?" Amy asked.

Julius lifted himself onto the rock and sat beside her.

"Nothing. Watched TV."

"Do you want to know what I did?"

"Not really," he said and laughed.

Amy's smile sank.

"Okay, what did you do?"

"My mom took me shopping in Anchorage."

Julius nodded. About a week after Julius arrived Amy stopped wearing overalls and her brother's Seahawks sweatshirt, which on her looked like a nightgown. She started wearing tight t-shirts that accentuated her chest and jean shorts that showed off the curve of her butt.

"I got new underwear."

"Really?" he said. "You wearing it?"

He noticed for the first time that she was wearing a pink bra, the straps sticking out from under her white tank top. Amy nodded. Julius put his hand on her thigh and fumbled his way to the button of her shorts, trying for a peek. She stopped his hand and shook a finger at him.

"You need to learn some manners, J-Bird."

Julius turned back to the river.

"Don't pout," Amy said.

"I'm not pouting." He slid off the rock, into the river. "I'm not a baby."

"Don't be mad."

"I'm not." Julius splashed through the river, found his socks and pulled them over his wet feet. He slipped on his shoes, and started walking north, toward the road and his dad's house.

"J-Bird," Amy shouted after him.

He heard her splash into the water. Keep cool, he thought. He quickened his pace and by the time she caught up he had reached the road.

"Julius," she said, the first time she had ever used his actual name. "You don't have to get pissed. We were having fun."

"I'm not pissed," Julius said, stopping in the middle of the road for a moment, looking at his feet the whole time. "I'm going to the barn. I'm tired of the river."

He crossed the road, listening to Amy's footsteps close behind. The grass stood waist-high behind his father's barn. Julius sat, leaning his back against the fading red wall. Amy sat facing him, her legs just inches from his own. He picked at the long blades of grass, feeling her stare like it was being filtered down the barrel of his father's shotgun.

"Do you like me, Julius?" Amy's cheeks tightened, her mouth pursed.

Julius split blades of grass in half with his forefingers.

"Of course I like you," he said. "I wouldn't hang out with you if I didn't."

"More than a friend?"

"I try to kiss you don't I?"

His eyes were fixed on each new blade he dissected.

"Better than girls in Oregon?"

"I don't know. You're different."

"What are they like?"

"They aren't as goofy or giggly, I guess."

"Oh."

"I didn't mean that."

Julius looked around at the barn behind him, the unruly field that surrounded it. His father hadn't mowed the grass in the year and a half since taking a job as a mechanic in Palmer, which left little time to tend to the farm that had been Julius' mom's pet project.

"I like that you're goofy. Girls at home aren't as strong as you. Most of them don't have muscles."

"Good," she said, and scooted closer to him.

Julius dropped the grass from his hand, pulled a new batch from the earth. He wondered what Amy was thinking. She wasn't looking at him. Her attention had drifted to the right where brambles took up ten or so feet before the fence of his dad's acreage and to the river just beyond. Julius watched her face, her lips pulled tight and small on her face.

Without a word she turned and faced him, leaned across his lap to kiss him. She put her tongue in his mouth. His eyes widened, and shuffling his hands

across her back he said, "That was out of nowhere," gasping for air as her lips left his.

Julius felt her eyes fixed on him as she perched on her knees. He sucked in a large breath and held it an extra moment in his lungs.

Julius kept his hands at his sides when Amy came back for another kiss. She kept her eyes closed. He couldn't help thinking she looked pained. He thought about the boys back at school in Portland, what they would say. He shifted in the dirt. Amy reached for the bottom of his shirt, he lifted his arms and she pulled it over his head, tossed it to the side.

"Where'd this come from?" she asked, running her fingers over the bruise that circled Julius' shoulder.

"My dad's shotgun," Julius said, and then, "Kicks like a mule," mimicking what his father had said the first time they shot together. His dad always held him by the shoulders when he shot, to absorb the buck. Julius was too small, his dad said.

"Does it hurt?" Amy poked gently at the black, blue, and yellow skin.

"No," Julius said, recoiling at the touch.

Amy kissed the bruise, twice. She straightened up and peeled off her own shirt, her hands shaking, and

revealed the pink bra and more muscles. Julius uprooted his hands from the ground at his sides. When he placed them over her breasts, her heart pounded against his fingertips. She took his hands away from her chest and held them tightly in her own.

Julius got to his knees and leaned over her. He ran his fingers up her leg and to the fly of her shorts.

"Not yet," she said, and placed her hand over his, clamping it to her waist.

He leaned down and they kissed again. Her lips no longer trembled and her eyes stayed open. She released his hand and he ran it up her side.

"We don't have to," Julius said.

His hands shook as he touched her face and kissed her cheek.

"I want to," she said.

"You sure?"

He leaned on his elbow at her side, his head level with her chest so he had to arch his neck to look at her face.

"I'm just nervous."

"Me too," he said, and let out a half-gasp, half-laugh.

She took his hand and led it back to her shorts. He watched her chest heave as he fumbled with the button. Her underwear matched the bra, vibrant against the grass they had trampled. He had a hard time with his own shorts, too, rushing to shove them down his legs. The compass knocked against his knee as his legs shivered. He kissed the curve of her chest above the edge of her bra.

"Is this okay?" he asked, breathless.

Amy nodded, her eyes half-closed but still looking at Julius' face pressed to her skin.

"You're beautiful," he said, first quietly, and a second time louder.

Amy smiled. She leaned to the side and reached back, unhooking her bra, her breasts firm, nipples surrounded by goosebumps. He touched them, pressed his lips to them, as she ran her fingers through his crew cut. The grass prickled Julius' bare thighs. He shifted and pressed tightly against Amy.

"Are you scared?" she asked.

"I feel tingly."

A laugh sputtered from her mouth and her body shook in his arms. His hands grasped her strongly. Julius moved back to her waist and he pulled her

underwear down her legs, as if he might seize up, have a heart attack. Her pubic hair was wild and stuck out like straw.

He planted his arms firmly on either side of her head and held himself above her. She reached between his legs and touched him, her eyes unblinking.

"Are you ready?" he asked.

She nodded and exhaled, then pulled her hand away, resting it on his back. Julius struggled to push himself inside. It made him think about health class. All the boys in class erupted when they were shown diagrams of a female body. "I'd hit that," one of them had said, while another chimed in with, "Looks better in person." When Julius slid in, Amy winced and pulled him closer. He tried to meet her eyes, but couldn't.

"Can you go slower?" Amy asked.

Julius relaxed, kept his eyes on the dirt and grass beside her body.

"That all right?" he asked.

Amy flexed her body upward into his chest. He felt her nod slowly against his neck, her hair brushing his chin.

Holding himself above her gnawed at his shoulder, like bone might break through skin. His arms wobbled.

Amy let out a painful squeal, and Julius finally looked at her. Her face was pale, the skin tight around her high cheekbones and her lips drained of color, almost matching the rest of her skin. He pulled back. She turned her head and he couldn't see if her eyes were open.

He sat back in the grass, leaned down and put his head on her stomach. Amy reached down and touched herself, when she pulled her fingers back they were tinged with red. She shivered and wiped them in her pubic hair. Julius couldn't stop looking. For a moment he was staring at Cash again, all blood-matted fur and death. He tried to blink the vision away.

He hadn't meant to shoot the dog. He just wanted to take target practice like he and his father had done when his parents were still making a go of it, their marriage and the farm. He aimed for a tree trunk, but his father had been right when he said Julius wasn't strong enough to control the shotgun. The recoil knocked him on his back.

Cash was off his leash and running east of the barn when the gun fired, now he lay three feet from the tree, a hole in his side, fur torn by the spread of buckshot.

Julius dropped the shotgun, fell to his knees, and grasped a handful of Cash's blood-streaked fur.

"My father's going to kill me," Julius said.

"No one has to know." Amy placed her hand on his chest and Julius watched her hand rise and fall with his breathing.

"He'll send me back to Oregon."

"I'm not going to tell anyone, J-Bird."

The grass tickled his skin and Julius shifted. He clasped Amy's hand between his, lifted it to his mouth and kissed her fingers.

"It was an accident."

"It will be okay," she said.

Amy covered her face with her hands. Julius moved up, scratching his thighs against the dirt, took her in his arms, and held her head against his chest. He stared past Amy, past the side of the barn, past the road, and the riverbank on the other side where Cash lay.

NOTHING BUT THE DEAD AND DYING

Sarah pulled the pregnancy test from the box, the fourth one that morning. Her best friend Ella had brought two more. They all said the same thing. Fuck.

Tug had been calling every day for two weeks. Sarah hadn't answered even once. Or any of his text messages. Even the ones with pictures of his dick. Especially those. She didn't want to tell him she was seeing his best friend Holt and Holt didn't have the balls to tell Tug himself. Instead, Holt met up with Tug every time he called. They smoked crystal together and played Skee-Ball or shot air rifles at Wild Bill's collections of signs that were plastered to broken down, rotting trucks.

To make up for not being man enough to come clean Holt had been stealing meth from Tug and bringing it back to Sarah. So, at least she had been getting something out of it. But now there was no telling if the father was Holt or Tug.

"This can't be happening," Sarah said, squeezing out a couple drops of piss.

x x x

Tug woke up laying in a snowbank, not remembering a goddamn thing. He could feel the high having evacuated his body like a ghost. It was snowing, each flake a star against the black night. He looked in all directions trying to remember where he was, how he'd gotten there. He was lucky he hadn't gotten frostbite.

He retraced his steps.

Buying meth from his Uncle Pete. Smoking it in his '85 Ford pickup outside the Wasilla Arcade. Calling Holt and telling him to get his ass to the arcade, though maybe Tug had done that before smoking the meth. Calling Sarah who hadn't picked up her damn phone in two weeks, like she was going to hold firm and not speak to him or something. Tug was certain that came after he got high, because he remembered what he did after leaving her a nasty voicemail: he pulled his cock out of his pants, imagined holding her down by her shoulders or squeezing her tits and took a picture with his phone and texted it to her.

Holt eventually showed up and knocked on the window of the truck. Tug unlocked the door so Holt could get in, and they smoked. After that they went in the arcade and bought a handful of tokens. The place was filled with old pinball machines and Mrs. Pacman. Tug and Holt played Skee-Ball. That's as far as Tug remembered.

He stood and his body ached with cold. He stomped his feet and slammed his bluing hands against his chest to warm himself. He didn't see his truck anywhere. It was probably still in the arcade parking lot. There were sirens in the distance. Sometimes it seemed the sirens in Wasilla were never-ending. Then again it seemed the meth cookers and addicts outnumbered the police. It wasn't that way when Tug was a kid. Back then all the cops had to worry about were the militia wackos. And the occasional freakout from Wild Bill.

Tug was feeling less disoriented. The street looked familiar, and if he was right he was less than a mile from the strip mall where the arcade was. He patted his pockets hoping he had his pipe on him, but found nothing except three arcade tokens. He must have left his keys in the truck again. He'd already had to bust out a window once this week. He didn't have any money to fix it again, which meant he'd have to cover it with duct tape.

His mouth was dry. Like cotton. His skin itched. He grabbed a handful of dirty snow from the side of the road and sucked on it. He started walking back toward town.

x x x

Pete didn't wear his false teeth when cooking. He finished bringing in the firewood he'd chopped, then took his teeth out and put them in a glass of water in the bathroom. After the last fire, the one that blew out the windows in the garage door, he'd grown more superstitious when it came to production. His son had gone to jail that night. Out on bail two days later, Pete Jr. died when he fell asleep at the wheel and hit a patch of black ice.

The smell of ammonia filled the house. Pete only noticed it when he came in from outside. He had learned to cook from his brother, Kevin who was serving ten years in Wildwood. For six years they had made meth together. And a good bit of money. Pete had thought about bringing his nephew, Tug into the business to take his father's place, but Tug was an idiot. No head for anything, let alone cooking. And he couldn't be trusted to sell it, either. That would just be providing Tug and his friends with free meth. All Pete could do was give Tug a better price. Partly because he was family, partly because Pete felt guilty that Kevin was in prison.

Pete tossed the logs onto the pile by the fireplace, then went into the garage. It was time to cook.

Holt knew Sarah was pregnant. Her best friend, Ella, had spilled the beans. He was receiving a play-by-play from Ella via text of Sarah's pregnancy test bonanza. Sarah didn't know Holt had been fucking her best friend. Holt wanted to be the dad. Tug would be a shit father, and sure Holt was messing around with Ella, but he loved Sarah.

"Let's hope it's Tug's," a message from Ella said.

Holt didn't know what to text back. Another message came in. It was Tug.

"Smoke?"

Holt had promised Sarah he'd be the one to break the news of their relationship to Tug, but he hadn't done it yet. Every time he and Tug smoked together Holt tried to summon the courage. What if he told Tug that Sarah was pregnant and Holt was the father? There'd be no reason for a paternity test, Tug wouldn't question it.

"Where you at?" he replied to Tug.

"She's taking her fifth test," Ella said.

"Arcade."

"Jesus," Holt said, then realized he sent the reply to Tug instead of Ella.

"What?"

"Never mind, bro."

Holt started a message to Ella, then deleted it. He wondered if Sarah would tell him or Tug first.

"You there?" Ella said.

"You coming?" Tug said.

Holt stared at his phone, began typing a message. "Do you think she wants to keep it?"

x x x

"I have a cousin who goes to Colony," Ella said, sitting on the side of the bathtub holding her phone in one hand and another test in the other. "She got pregnant her freshman year."

Sarah took the test from Ella's hand.

"Last one," Ella said.

Sarah held it between her legs. She must have had a gallon of water since she woke up. Sitting on the toilet with her panties around her ankles for what seemed like hours. She handed the test back to Ella.

"She heated a wire coat hanger and stuck it up her pussy," Ella said.

"Jesus."

"She saw it in a movie or something."

"Were you there?"

"No, she told me. She bled for days."

"Time?"

Ella checked her watch, nodded. She picked up the test and handed it to Sarah without looking up from her phone.

"Did it work?"

"Scrambled eggs," Ella said.

Sarah closed her eyes for a few seconds. She took a deep breath, opened her eyes and let them focus before looking at the test. Fuck.

THE PIT BULL'S TOOTH

What I remember most is the pit bull's tooth he wore on fishing line around his neck. I'd heard of shark's tooth necklaces, seen it in movies. A California surfer thing. And I'd had friends, natives, who told me about the bear's teeth and eagle talons their grandparents kept, but Buddy was something else entirely. A kind of man I'd never met. He was my mother's boyfriend during the summer of '07, her first since Dad had taken a job in the lower 48 and left us behind. I was nine.

Buddy claimed to be a stuntman in the movies, said he worked on three Schwarzenegger pictures. But not many movies were made in Alaska (it was cheaper, Buddy said, to shoot in Montana and pretend it was

Alaska), and he never went anywhere for work. Mom didn't question him, though.

The first time he showed me the tooth he told me he'd taken it right out of the dog's mouth. "The cameras were rolling and everything," he said. I'm ashamed to say the story gave me chills, made me crave adventure.

That was how our mornings went, after my mother had left for her job answering phones at a cannery. He would put me on his lap, ask me if I wanted to hear about movies. But I always asked about the tooth and Buddy always told a different story.

The first time Buddy touched me between the legs, he said the tooth really belonged to my mom. "She's the pit bull," he said. He held the tooth between his fingers. "This is how I taught her not to bite," he mimed the act of pulling it from her mouth. There was beer on his breath, thicker than my mom's perfume got around the middle of the month. "But you're not a biter, are you?"

His hand was warm against my leg, but still I shivered deep in my spine. He didn't say anything as his fingers worked their way up my thigh, just exhaled against my neck. I sat still as I could. As he pushed one inside of me he whispered, "It's okay" and "It won't hurt long."

But it did hurt, his fingers were callused and his nails untrimmed. The sweat he worked up made me sick. Mom gave into him, treated him like the king of our apartment, I was just another piece of our lives that he owned. I waited for him to go on his afternoon beer run before I sat in the shower until the water went cold, until the the goosebumps ached. Until I was so cold I couldn't feel the ghost trails of his touch.

After that first time he didn't wait for me to ask about the tooth any longer, just for the sound of mom's car leaving the driveway. "It won't hurt long" became "It gets better," but it never did. His breathing got heavier and eventually even his clothes, his skin smelled permanently of beer and B.O. The shouting at night between Buddy and my mom got louder, went deeper into the nights, and I knew he was paving his road out of our lives. I steeled myself, told myself he would be gone soon.

There were close calls. Days, weeks at a time we wouldn't see him, but it was three years before he finally left for good. I was a sophomore in high school by that time and other boys were starting to look at me the way Buddy did. Just a wrong glance could make my skin go clammy.

After Buddy left I scoured the apartment for the tooth, hoping he'd left it behind. It was easy to see he'd been telling the truth about taking it from my mother's mouth. He had broken her so well, as if house training a wild dog. How else could he have managed to keep us so long, so close? I wanted that tooth, wanted her to have it back. If she had been a pit bull before, she could be one again.

GUILT NAMES

When snow starts swirling it seems like the ground gets covered in minutes, like a blanket is being laid down by the wind. Dad went looking for the horizon when the last storm kicked up. Or maybe he couldn't keep waiting. Nothing good ever came of watching the snow. That's what he said.

Mom says to think of all the things that make me feel guilty, that tie my guts up in knots, and give each one a name.

"There's something about saying it out loud," she says, "makes you understand it better."

"Motherfucker," I want to say, but I keep it to myself.

All the names I know are full of hate. The kind Mom would wash my mouth out with soap for using, even if she thinks Dad's a no-good son of a bitch, too.

The road is dark and empty, and the weathervane on our neighbor's roof is turning slowly if at all. I try to guess when the next storm will hit. When the whiteout of snowfall will erase our driveway and the road that leads to it.

"I wish he was dead," I say.

Mom nods, keeps her disapproval to herself.

"I ate the last piece of pie," she says.

"I fell asleep in church."

"I still love him," Mom says, and takes a long drink of her tea, trying to keep me from seeing the storm she's watching.

VALLEY OF THE MOON

Nolan sits outside Sheila's new house, across from Baxter Bog, in the same Civic he had when they met. He looks in the rearview and runs a hand through his hair, lingering at the hairline, which isn't where it was when he last saw her. He should have called. But Sheila would have taken a hike.

She walks past the front window, turns and spots him. The guy she married comes up behind her, squinting. Sheila comes storming out the front door, her hand out like a traffic cop.

"Get the hell out of here," she says.

"I don't want to start nothing." Nolan throws both hands in the air.

"What do you want?"

Sheila's only a couple feet from him. Her husband is in the open doorway, starting toward them.

"I'm clean now," Nolan says. "Sober. Held a job eight and a half months."

Sheila's hand falls to her side, but her eyes are still fixed on him.

"What's going on?" her husband says, lacing an arm around her waist.

"I'll take care of it," she says. "Go check on Carey."

The man waits a second before returning to the house, craning his neck to watch the situation as he goes.

"What do you want, Nolan?"

"Just want to meet my boy." Nolan scrubs the top of his head with his hand.

"Five years you haven't been around. You didn't have the balls to be a spectator, let alone a participant."

"I know," he says, his leg starting to shake. "I'm trying to be better."

"Is this some kind of twelve-step thing? Amends, or whatever?"

Nolan shakes his head, shoving his hands deep in the pockets of his jeans. "I'm sorry," he says. Sheila keeps her stance firm, rooted to the ground. He knows she's not one to be suckered. Never was. "Look, no bullshit. I just want to meet my son. Maybe spend a day here and there with him. That's all."

"That's a lot."

He nods, takes a cautious step toward her.

Sheila folds her arms across her chest. She looks back at the house again. Her husband's watching from the window. Nolan thinks he sees the top of a child's head bob past in the background.

"He thinks Richard is his dad." She adjusts her stance. "Richard is his dad."

Nolan runs his hand along the back of his neck, turns toward his car. "I got it," he says, walking away.

"Let me think about it," she says.

Nolan, just opening the car door, perks back up. "Yeah. Do what you got to, Sheila."

"Hey," Sheila says as Nolan gets into his car. "How do I get a hold of you?"

He pulls his cell phone from his pocket. "Work phone," he says, waving it in the air. He recites the number like he's practiced saying it out loud. "Maybe I'll be a foreman one of these days," he says, and if he swells a little with pride, how could he blame himself for that.

x x x

Nolan gets Sheila's voicemail two days later, on his way home from work. "Call me back," Sheila says, straight to the point as always.

"There are going to be some ground rules," she says, ignoring Nolan's small talk. "But if you honestly want to be a part of Carey's life..."

"I do."

"Then I don't want to keep that from happening." Sheila takes a deep breath, the sound fuzzing in Nolan's ear. "We're not telling Carey you're his father. Not yet. Maybe if you prove you're in this for real we can reconsider. Until then you're a friend. Like the big brother program or something."

"Yeah," Nolan says, his throat parched. "I can do that."

Sheila sighs. A just-home-from-work, slumping-into-the-couch sigh. "You can come by on Saturday at eleven."

"Richard going to be there?"

"We'll both be there, Nolan. Don't start pulling any macho shit. You want to meet Carey, it's on these terms."

"Great," Nolan says. "I bought him a truck. A loader, like the one I'm driving."

"Nolan."

"It's bright yellow."

"Nolan, there are a couple things you need to know. Carey's shy."

"Aren't all five-year-olds?"

"He's more self-conscious."

"He'll be okay."

"Carey was born with a cleft lip and palate." Sheila says, her voice sounding older.

"It's okay."

"That's not the point."

"I just got home. I'll see you Saturday." He hangs up and walks into his apartment, flips on the lights. He settles into the couch, and turns on the TV, wondering about the cleft. He thinks he's heard it before, but can't place it.

The news is on, showing highlights of the Buc's game. He hasn't been to one since he got clean, worried that everybody downing beer after beer would be too much. But having his son there, that would keep him focused.

x x x

Nolan parks at the curb, five minutes to eleven. He knows Sheila will be surprised to see him early, probably at all. He shaved off two days of stubble and is wearing his best jeans--the only pair he's never used for work, and a brand new white t-shirt he bought earlier that morning at Fred Meyer.

Richard answers the door, hesitates before moving to let Nolan in. There's a part of Nolan that wants to lay Richard out, even though he's sure Richard's a good guy. Nolan takes a deep breath as Sheila breaks into the never-ending handshake and stare-down they've created in the doorway. He knows he'll have to share this at his next meeting, and he begins to sweat at the thought.

"Wait here," Sheila says, and disappears down the hallway. When she comes back she's holding Carey's hand. "There's someone who wants to meet you," she says to the boy.

There's a flutter in Nolan's stomach as he sizes Carey up. He's got Nolan's black hair. It certainly didn't come from Sheila, whose whole family has red curls. Despite the boy's downcast gaze, Nolan can see Carey's eyes and nose are all his. Classic Roman profile, with deep-set, but bright, blue eyes.

None of this surprises Nolan, he's spent countless hours putting his son together like a paper doll, changing out features instead of outfits. Carey finally lifts his head, revealing a strip of pink skin under his nose, a thick scar dominating his upper lip.

"Oh man," Nolan says.

Richard pulls Carey into his hip.

"What's wrong with you?" Sheila hisses, grabbing Nolan by the arm and pulling him into the kitchen. "What the hell, Nolan?"

Nolan looks back to the living room and Carey, whose head is buried in Richard's khakis. Richard's looking right at Nolan, making him itch. It's all new, he wants to say. There's no practice for this stuff. But there could have been, and that's what keeps him from saying anything but, "sorry." His cheeks burn as he nods at Sheila, who's staring a hole through him.

Over the fireplace Nolan notices a black-and-white portrait of Carey. The boy is smiling in the picture. That's all Nolan wants to see. That's what a dad should be concerned with. Richard looks at Sheila as she and Nolan return, but she shakes her head and Richard keeps his mouth shut.

"Carey," Sheila says, running her hand through the boy's hair. "This man... our friend has been waiting a long time to meet you." Carey's eyes are still fixed on the carpet. Sheila presses on. "Carey, this is Nolan." Carey looks up.

Nolan squats in front of the boy and extends his hand.

Carey turns his head away.

"It's okay," Sheila says.

A hand lifts slowly from Carey's side. Nolan grasps his son's hand, enveloping it, trying not to squeeze too hard. The fingers so small and soft, so fragile against Nolan's rough skin.

"You know what, Chief? I've got something for you. Hold on."

He bolts out the door and returns with the plastic loader he stowed on the porch. The truck's yellow paint is highlighted by red stickers on each side. Nolan kneels back in front of Carey.

"It's called a loader. An earth-mover. I drive one just like it. Here," Nolan says. "It's all yours, Big Guy. The bucket really works, too."

Carey bites his bottom lip and grabs the truck, lifting the bucket up, then letting it down. He makes a small grinding sound, like rocks being crushed.

"There you go," Nolan says.

"What do you say," Richard says.

"Thank you."

Nolan reaches out to tousle the boy's hair, but Carey pulls back.

"Carey," Sheila says. "Why don't you take your new toy to the backyard for a minute so Mom can talk to Nolan."

The boy doesn't take his eyes off the loader, but stands, wiggles a bit like he's trying to shake loose a wedgie, and walks out the back door.

"He's a little overwhelmed," Sheila says.

"You had a real piss-poor reaction, too," Richard says.

Nolan's hand twitches, might start shaking any minute. The anticipation is almost worse than the real thing. He looks at Richard and tries to envision his sponsor. He takes a deep breath and is mercifully saved by Sheila cutting in.

"We're done for today," she says.

"Can I say goodbye?" Nolan says.

Carey is on his hands and knees pushing the truck across the patio, scooping little rocks with the bucket. Nolan gets down on his knees, too. Close up, he sees the pink skin of Carey's lip. He wants to touch his fingertips to the scar, but keeps them planted at his sides.

"I've got to go," Nolan says. "Maybe we can hang out again?"

Carey doesn't look up at first, not until Nolan is at the door, and then his eyes meet Nolan's for the first time as he says thank you.

× × ×

Nolan was excited for the meeting. He envied the people who had uplifting stories to share. The people who had pulled their lives together, the inspirations. The church where the meetings were held was already open. He went in and filled a styrofoam cup with coffee before finding a seat in the front row.

× × ×

"Every kid likes Valley of the Moon park," Sheila said. "It's the rocket ship that does it."

So, Nolan sits on the bench watching Carey climb all over the red rocket, playing astronaut. "Your mom," Nolan had said in the car on the way to the park, then thought better of continuing the sentence. Instead he said, "Rocket ship park, huh?" and reached behind him, lightly gripping Carey's knee and shaking it. Of course kids like parks, he thought, feeling like the biggest idiot father in all of Alaska.

Carey crawls slowly up the rocket, like he's learned his lesson about gravity. Nolan waves from the bench. Carey keeps focusing on the climb.

The night after he finally met Carey, Nolan didn't sleep. All he could see was the boy's face, that scar. He looked up clefts online, must have read a hundred articles. He chewed piece after piece of gum, trying to calm his nerves. Trying not to blame himself, his genetics, for the countless surgeries his son went through.

And Nolan hadn't been there for any of them. He's trying not to think about it. Trying to enjoy the hour he's got with Carey. It's taken five meetings at Sheila's house, each longer than the last, for her to allow this outing. He even promised Carey they would get ice cream on the way home. Forget parks, Nolan thinks, ice cream is what kids like.

Sheila said Carey had hardly stopped playing with the loader and Nolan was starting to think maybe he was wrong. Maybe he wasn't just missing some gene for fatherhood. Even Richard had stopped trying to provoke him.

"Nolan," Carey says. "Nolan, I'm an astronaut."

His r's don't come out right, but Nolan barely notices now. Each time Carey says his name, Nolan is swept away, untethered from the earth for a moment.

"Best astronaut ever," Nolan says.

Another kid, a girl about Carey's age, comes running down the sidewalk from the hill above the park, darting toward the rocket. Behind the girl, a woman is pushing a stroller. She stops at the bench where Nolan is sitting. "That your son?" she asks, spinning the stroller to face her as she takes a seat.

"Babysitting," Nolan says.

"Oh," she says, as if he's less interesting now. "I'm Abby, by the way."

"Nolan."

"I guess you don't have any of your own?"

Nolan's keeping an eye on Carey who has climbed off the rocket since the girl arrived.

"No," he says, scratching his face, rubbing his hands across his mouth. "Just sitting for a friend."

A small group of ptarmigan march across the grass, and Nolan watches as Carey picks up a small rock, or wood chip, and hurls it at them. The birds scatter, their heads bobbing as they retreat.

"Don't torture the birds," the little girl says, and Carey hangs his head.

Nolan stands. Carey is clinging to the side of the metal play structure. Nolan walks to him and puts his hand on the boy's head.

"All right?" he asks.

Carey nods, takes a step closer to Nolan.

"Ready for that ice cream?"

"Yeah," Carey says, and it's almost a gasp.

"Ice cream it is."

Walking back to the car, Nolan fishes for his keys.

"Let me see," Carey says.

The one-year chip hangs from the chain, a white plastic disc with a hole drilled through. They'd passed it around the meeting the night before, like they always do when someone reaches another AA birthday, everyone taking a turn holding it, rubbing it, as if it were a good luck charm.

Carey sticks his hand in Nolan's. Nolan swings his arm, floppily.

"That's called The Noodle," he says and Carey laughs.

They pass the bench and Abby is sitting there, cooing into the stroller. Nolan catches her looking at

Carey, though, and his skin radiates. He flashes her a dirty look and swings his arm again to hear his son laugh.

x x x

Nolan checks his watch. He has five minutes to get Carey home, having messed around at McDonald's too long. They had sat in the parking lot, Neil Young singing "Like a Hurricane" and the two of them slurping the soft serve chocolate ice cream.

"You like Neil Young?" Nolan had asked.

"Who's that?"

Nolan pretended to be horrified.

"You are like a hurricane." He belted the line out, craning to look at Carey in the backseat.

"We've got to clean up," Nolan says, grabbing a napkin. "We don't want your mom seeing you like that."

Carey laughs as Nolan wipes the ice cream from his face, the scar. Nolan watches his son's face, seeing flashes of his own face from childhood photos.

"We'll have to teach you to play some air guitar, but it'll have to wait," he says. "It's time to drive and eat."

Nolan takes a big bite of his cone as they pull out of the parking lot onto Northern Lights. He flips open his cell phone to call Sheila and she answers on the first ring.

"What?"

"We're on our way, we stopped for ice cream."

"Pay more attention to the time, Nolan."

"Will do," he says and drops the phone onto the passenger seat. Nothing can bring him down right now.

When they park, Carey crawls up to the front to get out. He sits in the seat for a second just looking out the window. There's still a bit of chocolate on the sides of his mouth.

"You have fun today?" Nolan asks.

Carey nods.

"You going to have a good week?"

"Uh huh."

"Going to hang out with all your friends?"

Carey shakes his head.

"How come?" Nolan finishes running the napkin over Carey's face. Sheila is standing in the doorway, hands firm on her hips.

"No friends," Carey says.

"I'm your friend, Chief."

Carey looks up. Nolan thinks the boy might be about to cry. Maybe he just looks sad like that. He remembers Sheila always seemed to look sad. Forlorn, that was the word she used. She always blamed it on Alaska, the long winters.

"This place is only good for depressives and alcoholics," Sheila used to say.

"Forever?" Carey asks.

"For all time," Nolan says and puts his hand on Carey's head. "You and me. And Neil Young."

Carey smiles, the pink scar on his lip whitening with the stretching skin.

"Hurricane," he says, then, "woosh," under his breath.

"That's right."

Nolan's throat tightens, he can barely catch his breath. He reaches out and puts his hand on Carey's shoulder. He thinks about hugging the boy.

"You better get going," he says. "Your mom is waiting."

Sheila strides toward the car and Nolan braces for a scolding. She opens the door and Carey heads straight for the yellow earth-mover sitting on the lawn.

"Same time next week?"

Sheila shakes her head.

"We're flying to Seattle for a few days."

"Oh." Nolan watches as the boy digs up a chunk of the lawn. "Give me a call when you get back."

"We—I will," she says. "You've been doing a good job. Surprising, but good."

Sheila's talking the way Nolan remembers from when they were together, that slow way of getting the information out that makes him crazy.

"Richard and I have been thinking about leaving Anchorage. This trip is to look at houses."

The blood drains from Nolan's knuckles as his grip tightens around the steering wheel. His stomach feels empty.

"I'm tired of this place," Sheila says. "Have been forever. You know that. And there are better doctors for Carey."

Nolan nods. Sheila still remembers the car's fickle doors, how they don't close right, and lifts the door slightly to close it. Nolan gets out of the car, slaps his palm against the roof. Sheila turns around and Carey looks up from the loader. Nolan closes his eyes. He thinks about his counselor and starts counting down from twenty.

"I want whatever's best for Carey," Nolan says.

"We'll make sure you see Carey before we move," Sheila says. Then she turns and walks with Carey back into the house.

Nolan gets back in the car, resisting the urge to punch something. He bites the inside of his lip until his eyes water. He watches the front door for a moment then turns the key in the ignition.

x x x

Nolan sits in the parking lot of the liquor store. Has been for twenty minutes. The unopened bottle of vodka on the passenger seat is the closest he's been to alcohol in a year. He's sure he can smell it through the bag, the glass.

He starts the car and drives home. In the kitchen he pulls out a coffee mug, sets it on the counter next to the vodka. He walks away and takes a shower.

Drying off, Nolan stands in front of the mirror, steam rising off his skin. He thinks about how he and Carey have the same hair, tries to imagine what the boy will look like when he's grown. With his bottom teeth, Nolan pulls on his upper lip.

Outside, the sun still hangs above the horizon, but the moon is visible in the clear sky. Nolan plucks a couple ice cubes from the tray in the freezer and drops them in the mug. He unscrews the bottle's cap and stares at the sliver of moon suspended above the city. His hands shake as he turns the bottle upside down over the sink, holds his breath while the vodka pours down the drain.

He wonders how different the moon might look from someplace else. A place outside Anchorage, the valley perhaps, where a kid would have room to run. Where there would be plenty of earth for a father and son to move.

THE RUN

"This is the place, a real lucky spot," Dad said. "I've never shown anyone."

The banks of Spine Creek were silted with pebbles and the water ran quickly, but it didn't look deep enough to be a great fishing hole, let alone a hidden gem.

"You've got to see it in June. We'll come up around the end of school when the water's pink with salmon."

My father knelt in the pebbles, cupped his hand in the water, let it run through his fingers, like a gold miner in an old movie. "You'd swear the water was pink," he said again, "pink as a girl's..." he stopped and looked up at me, standing at his side. "Well, pink."

I was twelve then, in October. There had been a few snowfalls, but nothing heavy yet. And this trip, with the car packed full of fishing gear was the kind of thing Dad normally did on his own. When he asked if I wanted to come along Mom beamed and I nodded readily, figuring she had hounded him on my behalf. I crouched at his side as he dried his hand on his jeans.

"Watching those salmon run, it's something else. They're moving with a purpose we'll never know, kid. Never."

Then he looked off into the water, or maybe the trees on the other side of the creek. I felt the rocks below my feet, rolled them back and forth under the soles of my shoes.

Finally he stood back up, said, "If anything knows how to run it's them," in a voice so quiet I was unsure he'd said anything at all.

Dad set up the tent and unpacked our sleeping bags. He built a fire and made us some hot cocoa.

"Come up here in June," he said, gesturing with a tin mug in his hand. "Bring a girl. Not just any girl, the one you know you're going to marry."

My cheeks flushed at the thought. I hadn't even kissed a girl yet. Dad ran one hand over the other, feeling the divots and cracks time had dug into his palms.

"Bring a girl up here in June and fall in love," he said.

In the morning we split a Butterfinger and tried to skip rocks across the creek. My dad mentioned the run a few more times, emphasizing that we would be back. I tried to figure out what he did at the creek on his own. We clearly weren't there to fish. But mostly I was just happy to spend time with him. He worked in Anchorage and often stayed there during the week, rather than drive the hour south to be at home with Mom and me.

x x x

I was seventeen the next time I visited Dad's secret spot at Spine Creek. It was on a camping trip with my girlfriend, Julie.

Dad left my mother before school ended the year of that first trip. I think it was a relief for my mom, in a way. There was no more waiting. By the phone, or the front door. No more trying to balance single-motherhood during the week and Dad's weekend visits.

I didn't understand. I was angry at Dad for leaving, for my mom being okay with it. I started skipping school and stealing beer from the gas station's convenience store.

Mom never told me the reason he left, and I probably wouldn't have listened if she had, but she often said it had been the "right thing."

I've never seen how leaving could be right. I didn't hear a word from him until my next birthday, I hung up when I heard his voice. He called back and left a message on the answering machine.

I didn't like giving my father credit for anything, but he had been right about one thing, the run. Julie and I pitched our tent just a few feet from the creek's edge and sat on logs watching the salmon fight their way against the current, flashes of pink and silver flowing through the water like an echo of the northern lights. Looking deep into the water I saw the seeds of my dad's departure had been long in the making. That his retreats weren't just physical but mental, too. And that his admiration for the salmon was for their ability to pick a direction and fight with their whole life force to travel that course.

I've asked myself time after time why he brought me to the creek. Why after twelve years he decided to bring me to his secret spot in the world. Had he been trying to tell me something? That he was going to leave? Or did he even know yet? I always thought he must have known, must have planned it.

Watching the fish, I questioned all the logic I'd built for myself. Maybe he'd come here seeking answers and knew one day I would need answers, too. But maybe it really was about the fish. Maybe he had found a little piece of magic in the way the salmon swam the Spine in packs so large all you could see was the flash of their scales. Maybe all he wanted was to pass that on. To give something permanent and beautiful to his son before he left.

I looked at Julie and thought about the implications of her own departure and I knew I had instinctively brought her to the Spine for a similar reason. That my dad was finally passing on the moment he wanted to give me years ago. I stood, took Julie's hand and led her to the creek-side. I reached into my pocket for the ring I'd bought the week before; I'd worked all year to afford it. It was nothing special but it shined in the sunset like it was the biggest diamond in the world. My questions were answered, just looking at her by the water. I got down on one knee.

I couldn't help thinking of my father, the way he said he could feel the past and present washing away with the salmon, racing to lay their eggs. Running, to start the cycle again. Running, hoping only that answers exist.

GLACIERS

Gretchen says, "You wouldn't notice me if I was standing here dressed like a damn Eskimo," and Pike doesn't even look up from the grease-soaked Hog Brothers bag, or the Discovery channel program on global warming. She eyes him over the half-wall in the kitchen as she twists the corkscrew into the bottle of Pinot Gris that's been in the cupboard since they moved in. They'd never found a chance to celebrate. Even this, the popping of a cork, makes her sweat. She wipes her forehead with the dishtowel hanging on the oven door, looks back at Pike.

"I got pulled over again," he says. "F-ing troopers, hunkered in at the Eagle River exit like they've got nothing better to do than wait for me to drive past."

Gretchen pours a glass of the wine. "And what, you go downtown to pick up food instead of coming home?"

"I can't believe I have to drive out to the valley every damn day," Pike says. His feet in gray socks, still sweat damp, are planted on the coffee table. "When I was a kid everybody with a decent job commuted into Anchorage."

Gretchen walks around the kitchen counter, into the living room, and plops down next to Pike. "Is it too much to eat dinner with your wife? Maybe take me to Hog Brothers?"

"I just don't see why I can't operate a loader in Anchorage. I mean, it's great they want to develop out there, but that's a forty minute drive I don't need. And it's already cost me two speeding tickets."

"Nobody makes you speed."

Pike holds a hand in front of Gretchen's face. "Shh," he says, pointing his burger at the television.

"Alaska's glaciers are receding at twice the rate previously thought," the narrator says. Hearing this, Gretchen's skin goes cold for a moment. "There's another woman isn't there?"

"Christ, Gretch."

"Well?"

Pike crumples the take-out bag between his hands, throws it basketball-style into the kitchen. It hits the edge of the sink and falls to the ground. "It's no good," he says, and leans across Gretchen to kiss her forehead. "You've always been more than enough woman for me." He runs his hand underneath her, grabs a handful and squeezes. Two weeks after being cleared by the doctor and it's the first time he's even touched her.

"We used to screw like we were populating the planet."

"We're not teenagers," Pike says, sinking back into the couch.

"We're thirty-two, Pike. You make it sound like we're eighty."

"Most of the guys I work with go to the bars after work, don't come home until midnight. Or later. I come home, isn't that enough?" Pike takes a long drink of soda, until he's slurping at ice through the straw. "This is important shit they're talking about. Glaciers are disappearing all over."

Gretchen barely catches the sharp sweetness of the wine as she drains the glass. She goes to the kitchen for the bottle, tips it in the air. "You can't look at me anymore," she says. "Admit it."

"I do look at you," Pike says, but trails off, his words floating away.

"What? God damn it, Pike, just say it."

"I work all day. I just want to relax is all. Chill for a couple hours before I go to sleep and start it all over in the morning."

Pike's holding back and Gretchen knows it. Knows he's about to say how hard he works to pay the medical bills. "Let's get it all out there," she says.

"This is bullshit."

Gretchen waits, hoping he'll say something else. Anything. But he's talking to the TV, flailing his arms.

"Goodbye icebergs," he says, "goodbye ecosystem."

Gretchen shakes her head, she is exhausted, her limbs like rubber. "Who do you think cleans up around here?" she says, lifting the wadded-up bag from the floor. She takes another drink before walking down the hall to their bedroom, passing the spare room still populated by boxes that have yet to be unpacked.

When Pike was at work she rifled through shoeboxes full of photographs, and they're still strewn about the bed. She picks them up one by one. There are pictures of Pike and his buddies from high school on their trip to Cabo San Lucas. Gretchen's the only person she knows who's never left Alaska. Would she have done something different, gone somewhere new, if she had known?

She looks at her twenty-something face, her and Pike hiking the trails around Denali or at his softball games in the summer. He used to talk about bringing a son to those games one day. Teaching him how to stare down a pitcher. Eating hot dogs together in the stands after the game. Would he have married her if he had known she wouldn't be able to have kids? There's no point in clearing those boxes out of the spare room now, she thinks.

Would Pike have married her if he had known he'd be working like a dog to pay off the debt from her cancer?

She stacks the pictures in the shoebox, carries it back to the other room, kicking a pile of boxes on the way. In the corner of the room two cans of paint sit on newspaper. "Perfect baby room," Pike had said when they moved from their one bedroom hole.

"Where'd you go?" Pike shouts from the living room.

"Bedroom."

"You go to the store today?"

"No," she says, slumping onto their bed. She couldn't after those pictures, bring herself to do the shopping today. A mistake. A weakness on her part.

Pike is muttering, she can hear it even over the TV. She leans her head back and finishes the wine. Pushing herself to her feet, Gretchen sets the bottle next to the lamp and stands in front of the full-length mirror on the back of the closet door.

Her appearance hasn't changed much since the operation, except the bags under her eyes, which she conceals with makeup. She pulls her tank top over her head, drops it at her side. She cups her hands under her breasts, lifting. "Better," she says, watching the reflection of her skin, her nipples small blushed puddles. She unbuttons her jeans and steps out of them, one bony foot at a time. Then she pushes her striped underwear down her thighs, until they drop to her ankles. She runs her hand over the small fleshy pouch of her stomach, her fingers lingering over the scar.

Eight weeks and her hair has grown back. "There's no way," she'd told Pike, shaving herself in the bath the morning of the surgery, "that a bunch of doctors are going to see me full bush." Now she runs her fingers through the dark, wiry hairs, thinking she may never shave again.

She feels the swoon of the wine, her legs swaying as if she were on a boat, and turns from the mirror, leaves the room. Pike has turned up the volume. "With warmer water temperatures," the narrator says, "and the melting of glaciers, the global sea level is estimated to be six inches higher than it was a hundred years ago." Gretchen imagines the oceans rising, land-masses disappearing beneath gray tides.

The air is thick with the stale odor of Pike's sweat. He doesn't shower when he gets home from work, saving it for the end of the night before they go to bed. He just walks in the door, kicks off his Red Wings, and drops onto the couch. It takes the whole time he's at work to air out the apartment.

Gretchen stands a few feet from him, and at first Pike doesn't notice. Then her reflection flashes in the screen as the show goes to commercial.

"What the...?" Pike turns his head sharply. "What are you doing, Gretch?"

She walks between him and the television, doesn't even care the blinds are still cracked. She straddles Pike's lap and leans down, pushing her lips against his.

He barely flicks his tongue into her mouth, but Gretchen uses hers to pry open his teeth, takes his hands and puts them on her chest, undoes his belt buckle with one hand.

The show's narrator is back, and Gretchen is thankful Pike doesn't try to watch. She kisses his neck, then holds his face against her breasts until he starts to move his lips around her nipples. He holds her hips and she pushes herself harder against his face. He gets up from the couch, Gretchen still in his arms, carries her back down the hall, and lowers her onto the bed. He unzips his pants and lets them fall. Gretchen is sweating again, and she can't tell if it's a hot flash or that she hasn't felt so nervous since high school. Every touch makes her skin sprout goosebumps. Her heart skips a count or two.

Pike puts a hand on her stomach and she moves it between her legs. She's forgotten how dry the hormones have made her. She pulls his hand back and licks his fingers.

"Come on," Pike says, pulling his hand away. "Are you sure you want to do this?"

"That's all I want."

"Don't you feel," he says, but cuts himself off.

"What? Gutted?"

Pike buries his head in the sheets, nestling his hair into her armpit.

"How can I ever feel whole if people act like I'm not?"

"Just, what if it hurts?"

"More than being scared the rest of my life?"

Pike props himself up on his arm, kisses her nipple, even bites it a little, like the old days. Then he's up on his knees, positioning himself between her thighs. The goosebumps are back as she licks her own fingers, preparing. She puts her hands on his butt and pulls him into her, and for a minute it's everything she's wanted. Pike's rocking back and forth and she's watching his face, all concentration. He holds her tight and she closes her eyes, holds the edge of the pillow with one hand, her face dampening. She bites her bottom lip, recalls all those nights, afternoons, mornings, when they joked they would wreck every piece of furniture they owned within the first year of marriage.

Then she feels empty, like Pike's not even there, and he stops. She lets go of the pillow and opens her eyes. He's panting, sucking air. She gives him a light slap on the thigh, as if to say, "giddy-up."

He shakes his head, shrugs. "I can't, Gretch."

She wants to scream, tear the pillows apart, throw the lamp against the wall. "You have to. It was going fine."

"I can't stop thinking about it, you know?" Pike lifts her leg again and ducks under, lying at her side.

"How do you think I feel?" she says. "Sometimes I can tell where the parts are missing."

Pike kisses her shoulder, her cheek. "I kept thinking something would go wrong. Then I got to see you and..."

"And I was okay," she says. "Isn't that worth celebrating?"

"It scares me is all."

"It scares me, too." Gretchen runs her hand through Pike's short crop of hair. "We're going to do this right," she says, more to herself, and takes Pike into her hands until he's ready again and gets back on top of her. Pike keeps his pace slow and Gretchen holds her breath. He stays in motion for a minute before stopping again, and rolling off her. He faces the ceiling and Gretchen shifts onto her side, faces away from him.

"It's too much," he says.

Tomorrow Pike will be back moving dirt in the valley, making room for some new building. She's heard they're putting a hospital out there. State of the art, the Daily News said. Maybe she'll dig around for the keys to her old hatchback and drive out to see him. She hasn't left Anchorage, barely left the apartment, since they found the cancer, and Pike says the new overpass is finished. An overpass in the valley, they joked when construction started. Where could it possibly lead?

"We're receding at twice the rate," she says under so quiet, she's surprised to hear it.

"What?" Pike asks, standing.

Gretchen listens to the clank of his belt buckle as he pulls on his jeans. "Never mind."

Maybe she'll bring him lunch, like she used to. Surprise him with fresh steak or ribs. Or she'll keep driving to the places where there is no development, no dirt to move. She will find a glacier, where her skin can adopt the pale blue of the ice, still hard, refusing to melt for anyone or anything.

THE LAST FRONTIER

It isn't a blizzard, but that's the best that can be said for it. Summer is over. Dan had skipped right through August on this stint and summer in the Arctic is lucky to last through July.

Dan takes fingernail scissors in one hand and a pinch of beard between the fingers of the other. He moves quickly, roughly trimming six weeks of facial hair. Then he rinses the razor under the sink, takes it to his cheeks and finishes the job.

There is no guarantee the plane will be able to take off. There never is.

He packs the shaving kit in his Army-style duffel bag and fastens it shut, slings it over his shoulder and hoists his Craftsman toolbox. Night-shifters are sleeping and his own crew is already at the pump station. It's weird, even after all his years on the job, to think they can operate without him. Like he is a substitute running back getting a breather, then coming back into the game for a couple plays. He pushes open the exit door at the end of the hall, digs keys from the pocket of his best jeans, the ones he saves for going home.

The Deadhorse airport is packed. Fifty, maybe sixty-five guys, their duffels, suitcases, backpacks, toolboxes and tool belts. The chatter is minimal, but deafening. In the middle of the room Dan sets down his tools and pulls out his cell phone. He calls Terry to let her know he won't make it back tonight.

Maybe she's already filled the flat-bottom freezer in the garage. The cement is so cold her ankle bones ache. Between the roasts, ribs, ground hamburger, and steaks she could reconstruct a cow.

Maybe she's stocked the fridge with Amstel Light and the cupboard with a half-gallon of whiskey, removed the decorative pillows from the bed and couch.

Maybe she describes the ritual of his returns to a friend as being like making sure you get rid of pictures of exes before you bring your new boyfriend home.

Terry even takes Dan's truck to be washed, though their getaways to Portage Glacier or Denali are a thing of the past. And if he were to leave the couch during his time home it would only be to replace it with a barstool.

The call goes to voicemail. Dan looks around at the other men. Maybe Terry's in the laundry room, moving the bed sheets from the washer to the dryer. Dr. Fleischman, the therapist Terry sees once a week when Dan is on the slope, has told her to try and see Dan's visits optimistically.

Dan dials again. He knows she is excited for tomorrow, for her birthday and the nice dinner they planned. Now he is going to miss it, like he has missed so many other occasions. Terry will spend her birthday with a box of wine (in his mind Dan decorates it with a bow) and watching *You've Got Mail*.

Until she answers the phone she will still be preparing for his return. She will pull open her underwear drawer and shift the white cotton pairs to the bottom, the silkier, more colorful, skimpy panties to the top. Maybe she has stopped thinking of Dan as a husband, viewing him as more of an infrequent caller. A friend with benefits and a joint bank account. He wonders if she has a vibrator that she takes out from under the bed and stashes in a shoebox in the closet.

Lastly she'll replace the pastel towels in the guest bathroom with the brown set and pile the latest issues of Popular Mechanics and Hot Rod on the counter next to the toilet. On top will be the Sports Illustrated Swimsuit Edition. It's her way of saying they don't have to fuck every night he's home.

x x x

The flight's late, but Dan has finally made it out of Deadhorse and is walking through the Anchorage airport, duffel slung across his shoulder. He stops in the men's room and takes out his electric razor to clean up what stubble has grown since he was originally supposed to leave the slope. He ducks into the duty free shop and buys a small stuffed animal. A polar bear. It has a red scarf around its neck that says, "Alaska." The kind of crap a tourist would buy. Terry has probably filled the crib with a zoo of stuffed animals, but one more can't hurt.

Dan heads through baggage claim and hails a taxi. He gives the driver his address and, settling into his seat, tries calling Terry again, to no answer.

Dan closes his eyes, the movement of the cab lulls him to the brink of sleep. Maybe, after he called to say he wasn't going to make it home, Terry turned down several offers from friends to take her out.

And now it is Thursday. But sometimes these delays go on a week. Longer. The weather on the slope is that unpredictable. It can be a hundred below with wind chill one day and twenty degrees the next. One day a blizzard, the next sunshine. And sometimes a blizzard just lasts for days. So maybe Terry shuts off her phone.

Traffic isn't bad, it's well after rush hour. Dan's tried Terry's cell phone and the home phone twice each. He looks at the black eyes of the bear.

Since Terry first told him she was pregnant, Dan has considered quitting, though he hasn't mentioned it to her. He knows it wouldn't be hard for him to find work in Anchorage. Or at the furthest, the valley. He has worked for North Star long enough he could probably convince them to give him a desk job if he wanted. He would miss working in the field and though she wouldn't admit it, he thinks Terry would miss the muscles the job has cultivated.

Dan clutches the stuffed animal under his arm. He remembers reading that polar bears are solitary animals, that after they mate the mother goes through pregnancy and raises the cubs alone. Male polar bears are a threat to babies.

The cab pulls up to the curb. There is a black Lexus Dan doesn't recognize in the driveway. The outside light is on. As is the light in the bedroom. Dan forgets to breathe for a second, then nearly hyperventilates trying to compensate. He fumbles for his wallet and dumps a few bills onto the front seat.

After he grabs his duffel from the trunk, Dan taps his hand twice on the side of the car. He walks slowly up the driveway, peering into the windows of the Lexus. There is a briefcase on the passenger seat, a sport coat laid across the back seat.

Dan stands at the front door, grasping the handle while watching the cab drive away. He wants to take back all the scenarios he has concocted. He wishes he had quit his job the moment Terry found out they were going to have a kid. He grips the stuffed polar bear tighter, like a plush stress ball, turns the doorknob and walks in.

THE PIÑATA

I cleared the snow off the back porch, and rebalanced the pH of the hot tub. Ever since I'd signed the deal to create a series of training videos for a company in California I've had a lot of extra time. The job at North Star was supposed to be temporary anyway, but had lasted eleven years. I quit it first thing.

Juliette was throwing herself a party to forget she was turning forty, hiding the fact in plain sight by celebrating it. She put me in charge of the piñata. "Can I give you one simple task, Rory? Just one?"

I nodded, as was expected of me.

"And it will get done?"

"Of course it will."

Like the ice sculpture, we said simultaneously, recalling our anniversary party five years prior. If we were no longer in sync as a married couple an outsider would never know it from the nearly choreographed digs we took at one another.

Two days earlier I'd come home from my lawyer's office, having signed the final papers with the company in San Jose, the largest scaffolding manufacturer in the country, and found a condom swimming in the toilet like a tapeworm. Though my vasectomy had recently celebrated its third anniversary, I automatically wondered if I had forgotten to flush that morning. Regardless, we hadn't had sex in weeks. I pissed right in the center of the thing, driving it deep into the bowl.

"Fill it with those little plastic liquor bottles," Juliette said, still prattling about the piñata. "And maybe some little chocolates or something. From a boutique, not a grocery store."

"Will do," I said, plucking the car keys off the hook by the door.

I picked up the piñata at the party store. It was in the shape of a giant high-heeled shoe, pink and covered in sparkles. Juliette had this notion of herself as a character from a television show. A desperate housewife or sexy woman in the city type.

"I can't help it if I'm too classy for Alaska," was one of her favorite things to say. "Someone's got to spice up this iceberg" was another.

The man at the counter showed me how to fill the piñata and shrugged when I declined a warehouse-sized bag of assorted hard candies.

Juliette had always been high-maintenance, since we first met in high school, and probably before that, too. But back then we had paired off like magnets, she a cheerleader, me the tight end of the football team. It took time to shed those roles, or maybe adapt them to life as adults. She could probably still pull off any of those old cheer moves, and I wouldn't have minded seeing her in the outfit again, but I suppose my own station had slipped a bit. There was no way I'd be on a football field again, not without pulling a hamstring or throwing out my back.

I stopped at the drug store on the way home, bought every last condom on the shelf, and had a clerk check the back for more. I sat in the car filling the empty womb of the high heel with Juliette's newly preferred choice of birth control.

"Done?" Juliette said when I walked in the door.

I held the piñata like a halibut I'd just hauled out of the ocean. "Done," I said and smiled, even gave her a peck on the cheek as I walked to the back porch to hang the confetti-decorated high heel from the eaves.

"I'm so excited," she said from the doorway. "Drinks, hot-tubbing, a piñata, what could be better?"

"Maybe a moose will crash the fence."

"Party starts in an hour, aren't you going to get ready?"

Juliette was wearing a slim black dress that ended half-way between her waist and knees. Her hair was up, held by things she claimed were not chopsticks, but looked exactly like the ones at Chang's, my favorite place for hot braised chicken. Her knee-high patent leather boots looked freshly polished, though she hadn't asked me to shine them in at least a year.

"Wouldn't miss a minute," I said, stepping off the ladder and giving the piñata a little push.

I stood in the shower with the steam filling the air around me, grinning.

My phone rang as I was buttoning a new dress shirt I hadn't worn before. It was my lawyer. He'd just gotten off a long call with the company in California. They had decided to pull the plug on the training videos.

"What about the contract?" I said.

"They had a meeting before the contract was finalized on their end. I'm sorry, Rory. They decided to go a different direction."

I sat down on the bed, suddenly woozy, like we'd already started drinking, and as the phone went to a dial tone I heard the doorbell. Juliette said I had quit my job prematurely; she would be ruthless when I told her the deal was off. Dividend checks were supposed to arrive in a couple months. I wondered if the money would cover the cost of a divorce lawyer.

Juliette's few friends arrived. They kissed on both cheeks like New York socialites. I never fit in with this crowd. Not even if I wore the expensive suit Juliette had bought me as a birthday present a few years back. Not that I tried real hard to blend with them.

Daniel, the husband of Sue, Juliette's best friend, was a professor at UAA. Communications. Which meant jack shit as far as I could tell. He cornered me in the kitchen as I mixed martinis.

"What's this I hear about you becoming a movie star?" he asked.

"They're training videos."

"That's it."

I swallowed. "Just signed the contract a couple days ago."

"Good for you," he said and patted my shoulder.

We ate fresh crab, trucked up from Homer that morning.

"Should be Maine lobster," Juliette said. "But c'est la."

She had some philharmonic or other on the stereo, and though I knew it would devolve into The Rolling Stones within the hour, likely "Brown Sugar" with the women swinging their drunken hips and singing along, each note from the string section felt like a needle.

As dinner languished Juliette sucked the butter from her fingertips and with a booze-infused smile yelled for everyone to get ready for the hot tub. I had always ignored the disrobing of Juliette's friends when we had them over for a dip in the hot tub, but now I looked at each of them before surveying the direction of Juliette's own gaze. Just saying, she did talk a lot about how sophisticated Daniel was.

I held open the backdoor as our guests tippy-toed across the icy deck, salted with kitty litter, to the hot tub. Drinks sloshed in their hands. We settled into the bubbles, breasts bobbing atop the water, chest hair drifting like seaweed.

The last time we had a winter hot tub party we took turns daring each other to jump out of the warm water and race through the waist-high snow to the back fence twenty feet away. The difference between then and now was the crowd. That time had been my co-workers, people Juliette detested.

"Daniel said you're in commercials or something now," another of the husbands said.

"Training videos. To teach people how to use scaffolding."

"I didn't know you were so creative," Sue said.

"Creative?" Juliette snorted.

Toes started fumbling around in the leg of my swim trunks, rubbing my balls. Juliette was next to me; there was no way her leg could bend like that. Sue was across from me, but so was Rhoda, a paralegal Juliette had met at a Pilates class. And, of course, Daniel was between them, but I couldn't imagine it was his foot.

The big toe wedged under my dick, lifted it, the toenail scraping against my foreskin. Neither Sue nor

Rhoda were looking at me and Juliette had her face in a drink.

"Maybe we should crack open that piñata," I said, at the same time not wanting to be the one to stand up, not until the toes stopped coaxing my dick to life.

"Me first," Juliette said, practically jumping out of the water. "Which one?" She held up the tire iron and fire place poker I had laid out.

"Lady's choice," I said.

She dropped the tire iron and swung the poker. A white puff of breath curled off her lips. The toes squished against my balls. The poker struck the shoe, which twisted and swung wildly, nearly coming back to hit Juliette in the head.

"Who's next?" she asked, hopping back in the hot tub.

When it was my turn I chose the tire iron, hoping its blunt edge would be less likely to crack the piñata. I wanted to be in the audience when its guts spilled.

Sue went after me. She missed on the first swing, but connected with her second, breaking the surface around the toe of the high heel. That was enough to get Juliette back out of the hot tub, nearly slipping on the deck despite all the kitty litter. She took the poker, and

Sue backed against the wall of the house. Juliette swung with her whole body. The heel broke off and the condoms spilled out of the hole and scattered across the porch.

I thought I saw a smile start across Sue's face, then Rhoda laughed, a high-pitched drunken laugh that speared the air and made me think of an icicle shattering on the driveway in the middle of the night. Juliette covered her mouth with her hand, bluing from the cold, and rushed into the house.

Sue was frozen by the wall, and everyone in the hot tub seemed to be holding their collective breath. Daniel was the first to stand up. He looked at me with that look of disapproval all good teachers have in their repertoire.

"Guess the party's over," I said, stepping out of the water. My body was engulfed by steam.

Everyone filed into the house, drying themselves with towels as they walked. I wrapped one around my waist and turned off the jets on the hot tub. I could feel Sue's breath on my back, warm for a split second, then cool against the wet of my skin.

"Look," she said, "the Northern Lights."

I covered the hot tub and looked up. The sky shimmered with blues and greens.

Sue brushed her breasts, barely covered by a bikini, against my arm. She had never so much as uttered more than a few syllables to me before tonight.

"Call me," she said and turned to follow the others inside.

I figured she suspected the same thing of her husband and Juliette as I did. The Northern Lights continued to spread through the dark sky; the kitty litter had encrusted the soles of my feet by then. The sliding glass door rattled behind me as our guests left.

I kicked softly at the pile of condoms, their disarray spelled out an ending to everything I'd known. I began gathering them in the towel Juliette had left behind. I picked up the pieces of the piñata, too. Between and across the condom wrappers, the bright shards of confetti and sparkles made their own pattern under the iridescent night sky.

AIM

"Nice cannon," Nick said. "Next time work on your aim."

We both held our sides, panting from the sprint for the ball. We kept walking the path toward the barn, tossing the ball back and forth between our mitts.

"You ever seen that wolf-dog Mr. Simmons keeps in his barn?" I said. Mom said it was nothing but a myth and Dad said even if it was the truth it was legal as long as the dog was no more than seventy percent wolf.

"That's just something the older kids made up," Nick said.

"Let's find out," I said. I was still feeling pretty big after that throw. Nick had never thrown a ball that far, I could guarantee it.

We walked softly around the barn, circling to the doors. We'd been told hundreds of times not to go on the Simmons' property. Dad was always cursing Mr. Simmons under his breath. But it seemed like Dad had cuss words for everyone these days. We got to the front of the barn and Nick peeked first, then me. We didn't see a thing. One cow and a load of hay bales.

"Told you it was bunk," Nick said.

I gritted my teeth.

Nick slapped me in the chest with the back of his hand. "Hey, I forgot to show you what I snitched," he said.

He ducked into the barn, tugging on my t-shirt. I looked around and followed. Nick was digging in his pocket and pulled out a crumpled pack of cigarettes. I could tell by the red package they were Marlboros, same Dad smoked.

"There's four left," Nick said and pulled a book of matches from his other pocket.

He leaned against a bale of hay and stuck a cigarette between his lips like he'd done it a million times. Then he handed me one. It was slightly bent and wrinkled. Dad bought hard packs so his didn't get crushed. I put the filtered end in my mouth, trying to figure how to situate it. Should I hold it with my lips or teeth?

Nick lit his and sucked in, immediately coughing out a puff of smoke. He took another drag, coughed a little less. Then he struck another match and held it toward me. I leaned forward and let him light the cigarette, but I didn't breathe in at first. I watched the red cherry burn a little and let Nick take a couple more drags of his.

"Next time we should lift a couple beers," he said.

I nodded, knowing how easy it would be to take a few of Dad's. I finally let myself inhale. My throat burned with smoke and like Nick I coughed a small cloud. My throat itched, but Nick was halfway through his and had stopped coughing for the most part so I inhaled again. I coughed harder. I bent over like I was going to hurl. There was a rustling of a chain and a yip. I swallowed hard trying to stop the coughing and Nick removed the stub of cigarette from his mouth, looking like a pro.

There was another chain rattle and Nick and I peered around the hay. The wolf was bigger than any dog I had ever seen. Its fur was almost entirely gray, but for one black streak down its back. Nick stepped forward.

"Don't," I said.

"Don't be a chicken," he said and took a drag from his cigarette. He held it between his lips and leaned down to pick up a stick.

"Nick."

He ignored me and walked toward the wolf, holding the stick out in front of him like he was going to poke it. I coughed again and the animal's entire body sprung into action, lunging forward. I dropped my cigarette, but somehow Nick kept his tight in his mouth despite falling backward in the dirt.

The wolf barked and lunged again as Nick was pulling himself up. We both saw the chain break and it was like slow motion, us looking at each other and then without a word we both started running. I could hear the wolf behind us, its paws sifting through the gravel. We came quick on the end of the driveway and turned hard.

"Go that way," Nick said, pointing down the road toward our houses.

I followed his directions as he ran into the woods across from the Simmons' place. It seemed like a good idea, splitting up, confusing our pursuer. But as I hit the road the wolf was on my heels.

I started to stumble, but it was still a ways to my house. There was one driveway between the Simmons' and where Nick and I lived. I didn't know who lived there, if anyone, but it was my only shot. Two steps up the driveway though I was hit from behind. I skidded through the gravel, the wolf was on top of me, its eyes starbursts of yellow as it drooled and darted its head toward mine. Its breath was hot and wet, and when its teeth hit my skin it stung like iodine hitting an open cut. I could feel blood running hot down my cheek and neck.

A holler echoed through the air and the wolf lifted its head. It stepped over me and arched toward the woods. There was another yell and the wolf took off running again. It had to be Nick. I pushed myself to my feet, rocks digging into the palm of my hand, and limped the rest of the way home.

Dad's pickup was in the driveway and still making settling noises. He was home from the slope for a couple weeks, which meant he was spending most of his time drinking. That's why Nick and I'd been playing outside in the first place. Mom didn't like me seeing

Dad when he was plastered. She thought I couldn't hear them yelling at each other or that I didn't understand why when she was mad at him she couldn't look at me, either.

"Looking at you is like looking at a little version of him," she said once, sending me to my room.

When I opened the front door he was sitting on the bottom step, red-faced and pulling off his steel-toed boots. He was drunk, just home from the bar. I could smell it on him. He'd always been a drinker, but since he started working six-week shifts on the slope getting drunk was all he did when he was home. I hoped his own odor was enough to keep him from smelling the cigarette on me.

"What happened?" he said, steadying himself on the wall and standing.

My cheeks were steaming and the cuts were starting to hurt worse than anything I'd ever felt. Blood was dripping off my chin and down the front of my t-shirt. Dad led me upstairs to the bathroom, shouting for Mom the whole way. She came in looking like she was seeing a ghost. She took over for Dad and dabbed at my cheek with a wet rag. The sink stained with my blood as the story rushed out of me.

Dad disappeared for a minute and came back holding his hunting knife. Mom looked at him with the same expression she did when he came home late from the bars, not knowing I was up and watching from the hall. They didn't say a word to each other and Dad headed back down the stairs and out the front door. Mom was fitting gauze to my cheek, saying we should go to the hospital, but I pushed her hand away and took off after Dad.

He was halfway down the street when I made it to the door, and I knew he wouldn't want me following him so I kept my distance as he stalked across the road and into the Simmons' field, just like Nick and I had earlier. I nearly stepped on the sheath of the knife, laying in our driveway. As Dad walked, the blade glinted in the flashes of evening sunlight breaking through the firs. He held it away from his body, arm straight.

The wolf was laying halfway into the field, panting. Even from a distance I could see saliva dripping from its mouth. I imagined coming across a wolf in the wild. Camping with Dad maybe, even though it had been a couple years since he had taken me. When he was on the slope he always promised we would go camping or fishing or hunting or to a ballgame when he got home. But he never remembered. I wondered if we came across a wolf while camping if Dad would have pulled out his knife.

Dad's eyes were locked on the beast. He didn't hesitate, but approached the wolf cautiously. As he got close the animal stood, lazily, as if it already had its fill of adventure. Dad reached out with his free hand and lifted the knife higher in the other. I wanted to yell for him to stop, but no words came. I couldn't watch. I looked past the blade of the knife to the barn. Nick and I were blood brothers from the moment we met, cutting ourselves with the sharpest rock we could find. When our dads were on the slope we were the men of the neighborhood. At least that's how we saw it.

Out of the corner of my eye I saw a flash of light reflect off Dad's knife as he brought it around the wolf's neck. I looked in time to see the furry body slump into the grass. Dad turned to me then, the bloody knife loose in his hand. His eyes were glazed over and bloodshot. The gauze on my face pulled and itched. The taste of the cigarette lingered on my tongue and at the back of my throat. I wondered if Nick had made it back to his house, if we would play baseball again tomorrow, or share a beer in Mr. Simmons' barn.

Dad stood next to me breathing heavy and sweating whiskey. His shirt was splattered with blood. I couldn't remember when I stopped wanting him home, but I felt it now. My blood surged and my chest was tight. I told myself not to cry. Dad hated crybabies. I wished more than anything that he would leave and never come back.

The wolf's chest was still heaving. Why didn't Dad put it out of its misery? When he took me hunting he preached good aim, and ending an animal's suffering if you missed your shot. I'd seen him break a moose's neck once when his shot missed its mark. I turned, began walking home, not waiting to see if Dad was on his way behind me.

LOVE AND DEATH
IN THE MOOSE LEAGUE

Patterson's catcher came out to tell him everyone at home plate, ump included, could smell the whiskey emanating from the mound.

Patterson threw down the resin bag. "I rub whiskey into my mitt for good luck," he said.

Patterson didn't know the catcher's name yet, but the kid's eyes were full of wonder. Patterson had seen the look a million times, wide-eyed fans looking for autographs.

"That true?" the catcher said.

Patterson took the ball from the catcher's hand. "You've got a face like a mule, kid."

The umpire walked halfway to the mound and cleared his throat.

"Now," Patterson said, "I'm going to throw nine fastballs in a row, then we're going to take a seat in the dugout, see if you guys up here know how to hit."

The catcher turned around and headed back to the plate. He squatted and put down a single finger. Patterson laughed, nodded. He fingered the ball in his mitt, turning it twice before letting his fingers settle along the laces. He started his windup. Stretching his arm behind his head, Patterson could feel his tendons stretch to the max, muscle on the verge of snapping away from bone. He let the ball fly.

The ball snapped in the catcher's glove. The batter didn't flinch.

"Ball one," the ump said.

"Fuck you," Patterson thought. He slid off his glove and rubbed the middle knuckle on his throwing hand, shoving his thumb into the little hole where there should have been bone. He had punched a wall in the clubhouse after losing to the Yankees in the first round of the playoffs.

He slid his mitt back on in time to catch the ball coming back from the catcher. Less than a year ago he was pitching in the playoffs. Now he was pitching in an abbreviated summer league. In Alaska.

Dear, God, he thought, please don't let the title of my life story be From the Majors to the Moose League. Not waiting for the catcher to put down the sign, Patterson wound up and threw another fastball.

"Ball two."

Patterson walked the first batter and the manager came out of the dugout. He looked more like a grizzled old fisherman, Patterson thought. Then again, he probably was. No way these guys could subsist on Moose League salaries.

"How drunk are you?" The manager said.

"Not enough." Patterson tucked his mitt under his arm, rubbed the ball between his hands.

"You want to pitch today, or you want to sleep it off?"

Patterson stared into the plaid lettering across the manager's jersey. Lumberjacks. He had been an Athletic, an Indian, a Red, even a Marlin for Christ's sake. Now he was a goddamned Lumberjack in the Bullwinkle league.

"Look," the manager said, "This isn't where you thought you'd end up playing ball. I get it. But you could have retired. If you want to play baseball, play some baseball."

Patterson slipped his glove back on and nodded. The manager went back to the dugout and the catcher put down a single finger. Patterson tried to remember how it had felt to be young, to love baseball as a game instead of a career. It worked until he was halfway into his stretch and every muscle in his body burned. Even his bones felt nauseous.

He released the ball and when he did he could feel it on his fingers that the pitch was going to sail. It went high and tight and the batter jumped back, falling on his ass. The catcher had managed to snag the ball, keeping the runner from advancing, and now he started walking to the mound.

"Jesus, you guys like to talk," Patterson said, waving the catcher back to the plate.

With his next pitch Patterson nailed the batter in the thigh. The kid walked to first as the catcher's eyes drilled Patterson with pity. Patterson picked up the resin bag, tossed it back into the mound. The next batter came to the plate swinging like he was planning to chop down a tree. At forty-six Patterson was probably the oldest player in the Moose League. Hell, he was probably older than most of the coaching staff.

The catcher put down the sign, two fingers.

"Fuck you," Patterson muttered and shook off the sign.

The catcher put down his index finger. Patterson went into his windup. The ball was a rocket right down the pipe and the batter whiffed. The catcher slapped the ball in his glove then tossed it back. Patterson started his windup before the catcher had settled into his crouch. He let another fastball fly for strike two. Looking.

Patterson's arm was loosening, he was finding a rhythm for the first time in a long while. It felt good, better than he remembered. He pictured his last strikeout. In that playoff game against the Yankees. Got the last strike on the high heat, a rookie whiffing like he was going to win the game with a single swing. The next batter was their aging shortstop. Garcia, Patterson's old catcher called for a curve. Patterson wound up and as he released the ball there was a pop in his shoulder. Garcia was to the mound before Patterson had even finished his follow through. The whole stadium was silent.

The ball was laying in the grass not ten feet in front of the mound. Patterson looked at it in disbelief. Even the ump was bewildered. It was a few seconds before he walked in front of the plate and called "ball."

It was all over the internet. YouTube. Probably before the game even ended. And then SportsCenter's Not Top 10. Patterson had watched every hourly rerun through the night.

"Hey," the catcher said. He was standing in front of the plate waiting to throw the ball back.

Patterson held up his glove. He took the mound, toed the rubber. Didn't bother looking for the sign, wound up and threw old reliable. Chest-high. The batter took a big crack at it and came up empty. Hearing strike three called made Patterson's arms break out in goosebumps. He pumped his fist a little, resisted the urge to make a big deal out of one out. It was enough to forget the ache in his shoulder.

The next batter was a wiry guy, looked like he should have been a kicker for a football team. Patterson went into motion and got two more quick strikes. One looking, one swinging. He repeated "got nothing" in his head. He put another heater at the letters. The guy swung. A crack broke the air as Patterson's right leg planted. He looked up as the ball whistled toward him.

Before he could get his glove up the ball hit him in the chest.

Patterson swore he could see his breath knocked out of him. But the ball had managed to bounce off his chest and into his glove. The ump called "out" and the first baseman was yelling something.

Patterson swiveled. The guy he'd beaned was halfway to second. He threw the ball to first for the third out. There would be a good bruise on his chest in a couple hours. Patterson did a slow 360, surveying the so-called stadium. There were maybe a hundred people in attendance and that was a generous assessment.

He'd made it through one inning and his shoulder was catching like a sticky lock. In another time, Patterson would have sworn he'd thrown a complete game. And then there was the quickly swelling welt where he'd taken the cannonball in the chest. But he could smell the grass. He could smell the musty leather of his mitt. It was love.

Before moving north, Patterson had contacted a real estate agent in Anchorage to set him up with a furnished apartment. What he hadn't been prepared for was an Alaskan summer, where the daylight lasted well into the night, making sleep impossible. He'd always struggled with insomnia and having the apartment lit up as if it were mid-day counteracted even the bone-dense weariness he experienced after a game.

He found a craft store in the phone book and there he purchased a bolt of thick black linen. He hung swaths over the windows and laid down for a nap. He slept through practice and phone calls from the manager. When he woke he didn't feel rested, instead his body felt like it had atrophied in mere hours. Lifting himself from the bed was harder than he ever remembered it being. Harder than after pitching a complete game followed by a nine hour bender.

Patterson went to the bath and turned the cold knob all the way to the right, sunk into the porcelain and shivered as the water reached his testicles. An old-timer during Patterson's rookie season had given him this tip. "One day you'll wake up and your body won't want to move the way it's always moved," the aging set-up man said and Patterson had scoffed. Now Patterson felt like he'd had a thousand of those days and they were getting worse.

The water warmed to room temperature and the goosebumps receded from Patterson's skin. His joints were numb with shock. Whiskey and cold baths weren't going to do a damn thing but numb him a bit, but it was better than facing hospitals, doctors, and chemo. It was better than facing life without baseball.

x x x

The Lumberjacks' first road game was thirty minutes outside of Anchorage, in Wasilla. Patterson, like the rest of everyone outside of Alaska only recognized the name for one reason. They were playing the Nuggets. Reigning champions of the Moose League.

Patterson still hadn't learned anyone's names. "Get some names on the back of these jerseys and I'll learn 'em," he'd said at practice. The catcher was sitting in the seat in front of him eating peaches out of a can.

"You need to show me your curve," the catcher said between bites.

"I'll show it to you when I'm ready."

"Have you thrown one since your surgery?"

"Eyes front, Peaches,' Patterson said. "You'll take the pitches I give you."

"At least you're not smelling like the drunk tank today."

Patterson slapped the back of the catcher's head.

Playing baseball in Alaska was playing baseball in mud, Patterson had learned quickly enough. The team got off the bus and waded through ankle-deep muck in the unpaved parking lot. The Nuggets were on the field taking grounders as Patterson and the Lumberjacks settled into the visitors' dugout. The field looked like monster trucks had been doing donuts all morning.

"All right, Little Sluggers," Patterson said, when the whole team had filed into the dugout. "Let's beat these Palin-suckling twats back to the stone age."

"You know, there's probably not a single guy on that team who's actually from Wasilla," the catcher said.

"Shit, Peaches, way to ruin the pep rally."

"Is this a thing now? You calling me Peaches?"

"Yep." Patterson took his glove from his duffel and slapped one of the catcher's shoulders, then the other. "I dub you, my little Alaskan catcher, Peaches."

Patterson spent the game in the dugout, cheering on his teammates by number or their team colors, red and black. When Peaches came to bat, Patterson rallied the whole bench into shouting the nickname. By the sixth inning even a few people in the crowd were joining in.

The Lumberjacks were up two going into the eighth, but their pitcher struggled in the bottom of the inning, walking two to start, then allowing a run-scoring single. As they batted in the top of the ninth, the manager came over and told Patterson to warm up.

"I just pitched a couple days ago," Patterson said.

"And you're going to again. We need that big-league arm to save us a win."

Patterson dug in his bag for his pain killers, then stood and started stretching his arm. He slapped Peaches with his mitt. "Let's go loosen the cannon."

Peaches wasn't in danger of coming to bat, so he was still in his gear. They went behind the dugout where a makeshift bullpen had been marked off. Patterson tossed the ball lightly, feeling out the two-by-four level stiffness of his elbow and shoulder. The nerves in his wrist tingled.

The Lumberjacks went down in order, only giving Patterson five minutes to get ready, but he wasn't about to plead his way out of the spot. It was one thing to settle for the Moose League, but Patterson wasn't ready to settle for failure anywhere.

"I'll be throwing the heat," he said, putting his arm around Peaches as they took the field, and for a moment he felt like a rookie again.

x x x

The reporter was late. Patterson ordered another whiskey. He was finishing it when a woman in a black knee-length skirt and matching jacket approached his table.

"Mr. Patterson," she said.

"You're the reporter?"

Patterson stood. The woman smiled and extended a hand.

"Jennifer Tisch. Anchorage Daily News."

Her hand was thin and cold in Patterson's. She slid into the seat across from him and took out a recorder, set it on the table.

"You want a drink?"

"Gin and tonic," she said.

Patterson held up a hand until he caught the bartender's gaze.

"Gin and tonic for the lady," he said. "And another whiskey."

The reporter pressed a button on the recorder.

"The Moose League doesn't get a lot of celebrity ball players thrown its way, outside of playing exhibition games against Team USA, so what brought a Cy Young —winning, future Hall of Famer like Floyd Patterson north to Alaska?"

"Good, lead with the easy ones," Patterson said, sucking the melted ice from his glass as the bartender brought their drinks. "Honestly, I never thought I'd be playing ball in Alaska. And I'm still not sure how I got here. Injuries, age, all the usual ailments I guess."

"You hear about a lot of players going to Asian countries when their careers end in the states. Was that ever a consideration?"

"Sure." Patterson took a long drink and watched over his glass as the reporter did the same. "Ultimately I would have played anywhere. If that tells you anything."

"Maybe we'll talk about life outside of baseball for a few minutes?"

Patterson nodded, ignoring the twinge of guilt for having been prickly toward her. She was just doing her job. He'd always had to remind himself of that with the media. And this poor lady was a reporter in Alaska, she probably wrote articles for every section of the paper.

"Did your family move with you?"

"I've been divorced for nearly twenty years."

The reporter mentally flipped through websites she probably pulled up five minutes before she left the office, rearranging her intel. Her eyes stayed downcast, embarrassed.

"You have a daughter, though, right?"

Patterson nodded. He didn't think about Cassie nearly as much as he should. He felt like an asshole anytime she came up.

"She's older than the divorce," he said, twisting his glass under his hand. "Product of Triple-A ball at nineteen."

"So, you're in Alaska on your own, to keep from hanging 'em up."

Patterson took a drink. Even a player of his off-field reputation could get a job in a broadcast booth or on ESPN these days. His agent still called him once a day to tell him as much. Then again, he hadn't told his agent why he refused to retire.

"I love the game," he said. "I wish I could tell you there was more to it."

The reporter stopped the recorder, then used her thumbs to pull her index fingers down, her knuckles providing a pop that satisfied even Patterson.

"My cousin's on the team," she said. "So I try to make it to the games when I can. I'm looking forward to seeing you in your element. Maybe that will be better than an interview."

"I'll brush someone back for you," Patterson said.

Patterson always got a thrill out of a woman saying she was coming to watch him pitch. It never ceased to make him forget about a slump, or anything else for that matter. He'd thrown some of his best games knowing certain women were in the crowd.

He credited his no-hitter for the Reds to a local beat reporter in Cincinnati who offered to remove a piece of clothing for every strikeout he recorded that game. It was midsummer, so he figured at most she was wearing ten items. To be safe, Patterson struck out twelve. Five more than he needed.

The reporter finished her gin and tonic. Patterson drank ice slush.

"Want one for the road?" he asked, already signaling the bartender by shaking his glass.

"I really should be getting back to the office."

Patterson looked at the Guinness clock above the bar.

"Almost five, won't you just be knocking off anyway?"

She smiled. Patterson hadn't been on the make in a long time, but it was coming back to him.

"Another drink and I can stop thinking of you as a reporter and focus on you as Jennifer."

"It's a little backward," she said, sliding her glass toward him. "But one more drink and you're going to have to buy me dinner."

"Deal."

x x x

They do not call games on account of snow in Alaska. Patterson learned this in the middle of July. Six inches covered the field and the parking lot. But as the team warmed up, tossing the ball back and forth across the white outfield and the umpires swept off the foul lines and base paths, a squad car from the State Troopers pulled into the parking lot with its lights on.

It turns out that while snow might not stop the Moose League, a dead player does. Peaches, who Patterson had assumed was being his usual self, showing up at the park last, had died in a car accident. Patterson dealt with the usual losses of baseball plenty of times in his career, trades, retirements, injuries. But he'd never had a teammate turn up dead.

The game was called off, and the players milled around in the dugout for a while before filing out to their cars. The few fans were long gone. Except one. Jennifer was sitting front and center in the bleachers behind home plate. She was on her phone, head hanging so that her hair all but covered her face. Snow fell around her, looking like sparks as they stuck in her dark hair.

Patterson gingerly slung his duffel bag over his non-throwing shoulder and walked to the plate. Jennifer didn't look up.

"You're either really popular or really good at faking it," Patterson said.

Jennifer looked up and she wiped her eyes with the back of her hand. "Okay, mom" she said, drawing the word out for Patterson's sake. "I'll talk to you later."

"Sorry," Patterson said. "Didn't realize... Is everything all right?"

She slid her phone into her coat pocket and stood. She stared at the field a moment, past Patterson. She started to say something, but stopped.

"Shit, Peaches wasn't your cousin, was he?"

"He hated that nickname," Jennifer said, laughing a bit.

"It was too good to give up." Patterson nodded toward the parking lot and they both started walking in that direction. "He was all right. I didn't get to play with the guy long enough, but he reminded me of Garcia, this guy who caught me the last few seasons."

"I need to head to my mom's," Jennifer said, and almost as an afterthought, "I better write something up for the paper."

"I'm coming with you," he said.

"Where?"

"To be with your family."

Jennifer took his hand. Her fingers were cold and Patterson held them tight, trying to warm them. They walked past her truck to Patterson's car. He opened the passenger door for her, then got in the driver's seat and started the car to let the heat kick in.

x x x

It was snowing again, lightly, on the day of Peaches' funeral. Patterson recognized most of the people at the graveyard from other Moose League teams. Several players from The Lumberjacks acted as pallbearers. The manager eulogized Peaches, whose real name was Francis.

Patterson had played with The Lumberjacks for over a month, more than half the Moose League season, and knew nothing about his teammates. Many of them were probably the same age as his daughter.

Everyone took turns putting a shovel-full of dirt into the grave. Patterson had only seen it done in movies, but he had never been to a funeral before. He'd been in the midst of the playoffs when his father died, and spring training when his mother passed. No one would have begrudged him a stint on the league's bereavement list, but he preferred to focus on the game. He had always focused on baseball. First and last. As long as he could remember.

Patterson took the shovel from the first baseman. He stood at the side of the grave, tried not to think of himself in the casket. He slid a baseball card from the pocket of his slacks. It was a Johnny Bench card. Bench was the quintessential catcher. The very mold for the position. Patterson tossed the card into the grave like a hand at a poker table, then took a big shovel-load of dirt from the mound at the foot of the hole. His arms burned as he held the shovel taut.

Despite the snow and near-zero temperature, Patterson began to sweat in the seconds between shoveling the dirt and dropping it into grave. His arms shook and he tried to hold them stiff. When he dumped the dirt the shovel nearly fell from his hands.

x x x

After the funeral Patterson and Jennifer sat in the car, watching the snow fall on the fresh mound of dirt in the graveyard.

"There's probably something I should tell you," Patterson said.

"What is it?"

"The reason I'm playing baseball in Alaska."

Jennifer looked confused. Patterson couldn't help thinking of her soft skin, how he would watch her sleep in the middle of the night.

"I want you to know I'm all in, chips on the table, everything," he said. "I've got bone cancer. Couldn't pass a big league physical if I wanted to."

For a moment the car was silent but for the whirr of the heater. Patterson watched Jennifer's eyes dim, shift back and forth, then focus. He could practically see the irises tighten.

"Jesus," she said. "But how are you playing?"

"It hurts, but it's going to hurt no matter what. It's either sit around and wait to die or do what I know how to do."

"Have you told your daughter?"

"I haven't even told my agent."

"Fuck your agent, Floyd. Christ."

Patterson could see Jennifer's mind was racing with a thousand questions, ideas, and plans to research things. Patterson knew that frantic energy. It was a trait common to the fairer sex, at least to the one's he'd found himself most fond of. Then suddenly she was crying. Patterson tried to comfort her, shifting to the edge of his seat so he could put an arm around her.

"Why haven't you told anyone?" she asked, wiping her eyes.

"I just want to play baseball."

"And die in middle of a game?"

"Beats dying in a hospital bed, hooked up to machines and IV's."

"Jesus, Floyd. Jesus."

Patterson hadn't been to Jennifer's apartment, but she had insisted he come home with her.

"I want you to see the article," she said.

She held his hand as they walked through the parking lot. He couldn't remember holding hands with a woman. It seemed weird, but he couldn't think of a single damn time. He tried not to wonder if she was only holding his hand because she thought he was frail. He focused on the feeling of her fingers laced with his.

In the kitchen she poured him a glass of scotch, handed it to him with a folded bundle of paper.

"I'm going to take a shower," she said, beginning to unzip her dress. "Make yourself comfortable.

Patterson sat in the living room and set his drink on the coffee table. There was baseball paraphernalia on all the walls. Framed pictures of Sandy Koufax and Nolan Ryan. Signed baseballs on counters, books about baseball in stacks next to the couch. Patterson didn't know anything about the woman he'd been sleeping with. He unfolded the papers. The article was titled,

"Love and Death in the Moose League." He knew it was time to tell people. His agent, Cassie, everyone.

x x x

It was twilight, the Alaskan summer clearly gone and fall skipped over completely in favor of winter. Patterson's season in the Moose League had seen more snow than all his combined years in the Majors. But he knew now why Alaskans didn't think anything of summer snow, because it was October and the very air felt different. There was nearly a foot of snow and he knew it wasn't likely he'd see the ground again for months.

Patterson walked through the parking lot to the field, letting himself through the chain-link gate. Even if he made it to spring, he didn't have another season in him. And he still hadn't called Cassie. They weren't on the best terms and he didn't want to seem like he was asking for a pass on being a shitty father because he was dying, but Jennifer wouldn't wait for the cancer to kill him if he didn't call Cassie soon.

He waded through the snow until he found the slope of the mound, and brushed away the snow as best he could with his foot. He turned a ball over in his hands, feeling the seams against his skin. He toed the rubber and went into his windup.

The ball left his fingers perfect, the whip of his arm effortless. He didn't need a radar gun to know when a pitch pushed triple digits. There was an ease, an elasticity, to the flow of his arm. It had been too long since he felt it. Like a sort of lift off, or getting a buzz from your first beer.

Patterson didn't bother retrieving the ball. He didn't want to throw again, he wanted to leave with that feeling of invincibility. He laid on his back in the middle of the infield, poised like a child ready to make a snow angel. The cold lick of the ice burned on the back of his ears and neck. His limbs went numb.

Beneath him was a baseball field, everything he had ever lived for. He inhaled, tried to find the smell of dirt and grass. It was there somewhere, he knew.

MAMMOTH

He sits in the bath, watching the hair on the mound of his stomach drift like pond weeds with every small movement of the water. He is hunched over, pumped full of pain meds and unable to concentrate on the tangible: his body tingling, but numb; his wife kneeling beside the bath, dipping a washcloth into the water, then ringing it out over his shoulders.

It had been snowing when they came home from the surgery. His wife had asked if he was hungry and though his stomach felt hollow all he could think to eat was French fries, so she pulled into a drive-thru.

Somewhere deep in his brain he was aware, overly so, of what had brought them here—he in the bath, her washing him. A softball sized tumor attached to the muscle under his shoulder blade. Mammoth, he had heard the surgeon say to another doctor. And though he was aware of this he could not formulate his thoughts into words, those catalogs of family medical histories and secret fears.

There was a time not so long ago that if he and his wife were in the bathroom together he was not the only naked one, nor the only in the bath. He wants to laugh about this turn of events as she rings out the washcloth over his stitches, which sting as the water runs over them, but he cannot seem to make his brain pass the message along.

When they had first arrived home, he asked her to take a picture of his back and for hours that night he stared at it, the purple-yellow bruising around the incision site, and the stitches, which resembled the laces of a baseball if tied with black plastic instead of red string.

The water had grown tepid and the sight of his dick shriveled in the water made him sad. Perhaps a selfish reminder that everything he enjoyed could be ruined so quickly. His wife leaned over the side of the bath and kissed his cheek. He knew she, too had thoughts yet to be given a voice.

His wife asked if there was anything he needed and his cheeks flushed, his eyes stung. He tried to breathe. Suddenly he needed nothing and wanted everything. He wanted nothing and needed everything.

MODEL HOME

I was making you listen to songs in my car, a mix CD I'd just made you. We were sitting in the backseat and you leaned over me so I got a whiff of your shampoo. Strawberry-kiwi. You hiked up your dress and straddled my lap. We kissed and you moved up and down a bit, rubbing on me just to prove you could get me excited at will.

"Let's go to the house," you said.

You had been working for a real estate company, showing people a model house for a subdivision they were hoping to build behind the truck stop south of Palmer.

"Let's sit here and listen to music," I said and kissed your neck.

You'd gotten accepted to a university in the lower 48, the University of Michigan. "At least the weather would be familiar," you'd said. I knew you were struggling with the decision of whether or not to stay in Alaska. To stay with me.

You kept begging to go to the house until I gave in and we got back in the front seats. You pulled down your dress and smoothed it out. I put the car in gear. It felt like a sledgehammer to my gut how badly I wanted to feel the insides of your thighs. How suddenly it felt like a matter of life and death. Having you, every inch of you, and keeping it.

We drove out past the truck stop into the overgrown field that had been leveled by developers. It was spring but it had snowed a few days before and the ground was still muddy. We drove through the fake streets, marked with stakes and neon spray paint so investors could envision the layout. There was one house at the back of the lot. I parked to the right of it, imagining a driveway.

"There's a generator out back," you said, looking at me with a big smile.

"I'll get it."

You kissed my cheek and told me to meet you inside. I trudged through the mud around the back of the house and found the generator. We'd been going together almost eight months, which was long enough that people were starting to have expectations about our relationship. Even my dad, who had been bugging me to get a job, was now adjusting his strategy.

"You can put some money away for a ring," he said.

Only I knew you were going to leave. You hadn't shown the letter to your parents, and you wouldn't have shown it to me, if it hadn't fallen out of your purse. You said you didn't know what you were going to do and I believed you. Still, there'd been a feeling in my gut ever since.

I was in love with you. Of course I was in love with you. That was the horrible, gut-twisting sensation I'd been suffering every time I looked at you lately. But I didn't even know what I wanted to do with my life. I just wanted to listen to music. Or play guitar. A few bars in Anchorage had already given my band some gigs.

I flipped the switch on the generator and grabbed the pull crank. I wasn't ready to start a family or have a wife or move into some subdivision in the valley. I wasn't ready for kids or a mortgage. I yanked the cord a second time and the motor sucked and caught.

A couple lights came on. You were there in the kitchen window waving. I didn't know what you thought about any of this stuff, I was too scared to ask. Too afraid you would say you were ready for all of it. Or worse, that you'd made up your mind about leaving. You opened the back door, stood out on the porch.

"Coming in?"

I walked up the steps, scraping mud off my shoes. You took my hand, showed me around like I was a prospective investor. You said things like "crown molding." I had no idea what you were talking about, but I nodded anyway. We got to the bedroom and I grabbed you by the hips. I hiked up your dress so I could see your thighs again.

"The room has a lovely feng shui," you said, reciting another line from the script the real estate company had given you.

I picked you up and laid you on the bed, crawled between your legs, pushing your dress ahead of me. You went on about whirlpool baths, walk-in closets, and adjoining rooms.

"Perfect for a nursery," you said.

I wondered if it was true that listening to rock and roll was unhealthy for babies. Just the idea of playing lullabies on my guitar made me feel like a sellout.

"I'm just teasing," you said, but the laughter had faded from your eyes.

I kept my eyes open as you pulled me down and kissed me. I pushed inside you and took my time, trying to memorize you like the chords of my favorite song. But you were too infinite to memorize, and I knew then I would give up anything. All you would have to do was stay and there would be no home we couldn't fill.

COMING HOME

Jared Deitrich, PFC exited the plane and entered Anchorage International Airport, the first time he'd been home since leaving for basic training four years earlier. The colorful sweaters and ski coats of holiday travelers made him self-conscious of his fatigues. His family was waiting at the edge of the gate. They were holding a sign welcoming him home.

Jared's father hadn't changed, his hair gray and trimmed only slightly longer than Jared's own. According to the last letter Jared received from his mother, his dad had cut down his time at work, but was still pulling four-week shifts on the slope.

His mother, though, who had long brown curls when Jared left, now sported a mangy gray cut above her shoulders. It was almost wolf-like and seemed to spread horizontally, like a permanent static was pulling from both sides.

And there was Jessie, his younger sister. She'd been eleven when he left. She was wearing the Army sweater Jared had sent back for their father, hanging like a night shirt. She pushed the sleeves up her arms and ran to him. Jared clutched her, lifted her as if she were still a child. His family, friends, and people he didn't recognize at all encircled him and the olive green duffel he'd set at his feet.

x x x

Jared had slept nearly twenty-four hours and was still in uniform when he woke. It was the best sleep he'd had in years. He unbuttoned his shirt and threw it on the floor next to his shoes.

The house was dark, but for the distant glow of the TV, which filtered through the hall from the living room. The pictures that lined the hallway, the furniture and their positions, were the same as he remembered.

Jessie was lying on the couch. Her pajama pants were printed with characters from My Little Pony. Jared remembered teasing her about watching that show.

"Hey, Brother," she said.

Jared nodded.

"Want to sit?" Jessie sat up, patted the cushion next to her.

Jared sat. His sister's warmth lingered in the cushion beneath him. "What are we watching?"

"The new Adam Sandler," she said, and Jared felt her eyes on him for a moment before she added, "Do you guys get to see movies?"

"Sure. Sometimes."

Jessie let out a small squeal, like an excited child. "What's that?" she said, looking at his arm. She pushed the sleeve of Jared's undershirt up to his shoulder. Her fingers gave him a small static shock. "A tattoo? When'd you get that?"

"Couple years ago."

She ran her fingers over the eagle on Jared's bicep for a minute before plopping her head onto his lap. "This part's funny," she said, pointing to the TV.

Jared watched her smile spread and open with laughter. It had been a couple years, at least, since he'd seen her picture. "We understand," his mother had said when he re-upped, but what she meant was that she understood. That she knew the memories coming home would drag up.

Jessie reached up and cupped his chin in her hand. "I'm glad you're home, Jared," she said, her eyes still trained on the movie.

"Me, too." Jared leaned down and pressed his lips to the back of her head. He tasted the coconut of her shampoo. It was surreal, after those years of babysitting Jessie, sitting here with her now, grown up. But it was instinctual, too, as if he'd had a hand in raising her. A momentary shiver slid down his spine. Not unlike the feeling he had gotten crouching behind the ruins of buildings in small Iraqi towns, uncertain from where gunfire was coming.

Jessie adjusted herself, and Jared watched the patch of soft downy skin on her lower back peek out from beneath her t-shirt. He started to put his hand there, or on her hip. "Got to pee," he said, and Jessie sat up, her ponytail frisking his face as he stood.

It could no longer be called sleep, what Jared did between sinking into bed, and the moment when sunlight first crept through the window. His eyes were shut, and images passed like dreams before his eyes. But it was not sleep. Sleep was a restful thing, and Jared never felt rested.

He saw a dirt road outside of Baghdad, stretching out into the desert. And himself, standing there. No one else from his unit around him. No Humvee, no tanks. Not a trace of the enemy even. It was just him and the dirt road over and over again. And there was always a voice in the air, a whisper. Jared had never forgotten it. It was the voice of Mr. Kansky, their neighbor when Jared was in grade school. It was Mr. Kansky's voice calling to him in the backyard, or hushing him when he'd put his hand down Jared's pants, or telling him to take his pants off. Mr. Kansky would put his cigarette-smelling mouth on Jared, tell him it was a game adults played.

By the time he woke, sometimes earlier than others, the sheets were, without fail, sweat-damp, and Jared would open his eyes and blink away the bright white, brown, and beige of the desert. Shake off the voice of the past.

Jared guessed it was about three a.m. He opened his eyes. 2:56. Footsteps. His pulse quickened, then he forced a soft laugh at himself.

The footsteps were in the room next to his, Jessie's room. Jared listened as they entered the hall. Still stuck on the road in the desert, he listened to Jessie enter his room.

"Jared?"

He sat up.

"Did I wake you?"

Jared shook his head. Jessie sat on the edge of the bed. She was wearing plaid boxers. Her legs shone, reflecting what little moonlight was breaking through the shades and the cloud cover. He could feel her body, pushing ahead like an Iraqi breeze.

"You remember the time I caught you and Olivia Root making out?"

Jared nodded. He had dated Olivia his junior year of high school. He had dated her because she had a reputation for being easy.

"I watched through the crack of your door," Jessie said. "I saw Olivia take off her shirt."

Jared shifted. He started to sweat, watching Jessie's breathing grow heavier, her chest rising and falling. It's just a touch.

"I saw you put your hand..." Jessie placed her hand on her thigh. It seemed she wasn't even talking to him.

"Why?" Jared asked.

Jessie looked up. "I don't know."

"You wondering about boys?" Jared's throat was parched, a feeling he had come to know intimately. The words were his own, but so close to words that haunted him.

Jessie laughed. "Don't worry, I'm not asking for a birds-and-bees." She shook her head. "Just a funny memory," she said. "Sorry I woke you." She leaned forward and kissed Jared's forehead, her breasts, swaddled by her tank top, were suspended in front of his face.

x x x

"It'll be small," Jared's mother had said. She had organized a coming home party for him. "Some family and friends. Everybody is just so relieved." Jared mustered a smile.

Of course it was more like half of Anchorage. Jared didn't even recognize the majority of the people who were shaking his hand or clapping him on the back. He stood near the stereo sipping a beer. His mom had put on music she no doubt thought was hip. Occasionally she would bring someone by and introduce them to Jared. Each asked how relieved he was to be home and told him how proud he made them. How proud they were of the whole armed forces, really.

When Jessie emerged from her room, where she'd sequestered herself to finish a history paper, she was wearing a jean skirt and a tight t-shirt. Jared found it hard to breathe for a moment, like the onset of a panic attack. He hadn't had one since his first tour, just one, on the plane as it made its descent into the desert. He vomited out the cargo door. But he could feel the momentum building sometimes, the acid piling up in his throat, the weight bearing down on his chest.

When he made eye contact with Jessie his breathing was becoming regular again. She smiled and half-waved from across the room. He held up his beer in acknowledgment. Their mother was there, next to him again with a platter of cheese and crackers.

"You need a girlfriend," she said.

The acid rose again. The weight bore down. "Why?"

His mother laughed. "I don't imagine there's a lot of time for dating in the army." Jared shook his head. "You're a good man, you need a good girl to look out for you. There's someone I want to introduce you to."

"Christ."

Jared's mother slapped his hand. "Mary's daughter, Megan is your age. She's going to UAA."

"No thanks."

"She's a real looker." Jared's mother winked at him. "Just meet her."

"Let me know," Jared's dad said. "If you want the job I'll make a call. Up to you."

"I'll think about it." Jared said goodbye and hung up the phone. His dad had been back on the slope for a few days, and every call home had encouraged Jared to take a job at the pump station.

"Shouldn't you be getting ready for your date, Stud?" Jessie was pouring a glass of orange juice.

"It's not a date."

"Oh, it's a date, Brother. Mom's still making play dates for you."

Jared waited for Jessie to finish taking a drink, then grabbed her in a headlock. "You think she won't be making them for you, too?" Her breath steamed against his hand and he released her as the hair on the back of his neck stood.

Jessie bent forward and shook out her hair, preparing to pull it back in a ponytail. "You going to go work with dad?"

"Not likely."

"How come?"

Jared looked out the kitchen to the backyard. "You don't remember the house we lived in before here, do you?" Jared's mother hadn't told his dad about Mr. Kansky, just bugged him about moving to a different part of Anchorage.

Jessie shook her head.

"I'm not sure I'm leaving the army."

Jessie put a hand on Jared's arm. "It's time to come home," she said, then finished her orange juice.

x x x

Jared met Megan outside The Inlet Steakhouse, and was pleased that at least his mother had not been exaggerating Megan's looks. Her smile was toothpaste commercial material. She couldn't be much taller than five feet, Jared imagined, after the heels came off, but even at his six two she didn't make him feel tall. He held the door open for her couldn't help looking her up and down the whole way to the table.

"How does it feel to be home?" She asked, leveling her eyes over the top of the menu.

"Weird."

"Sounds like it's been a long time."

Longer than you know, Jared thought. He scanned the menu, though he knew what he wanted.

"I know it's awkward to be set up like this," Megan said. "But who's going to argue with a crazy mother?"

"Not me."

The waiter arrived and Megan ordered a baked potato and a salad.

"Tri-tip," Jared said. "Rare, with fries."

"So what are you going to do now?"

Jared shook his head. "Guess I'm undecided."

Megan had a softness he wasn't used to. It made him uncomfortable, but he was glad he'd agreed to meet her.

"Do you like the army?"

"I know the army." Jared twisted his water glass atop the coaster. "Everything else is confusing."

Megan nodded. "We haven't know each other very long," she said, "but I think I'd like it if you stuck around." She reached out and put her hand on Jared's.

"Thanks," he said, and stared at her fingers, tried not to picture Jessie.

"Jared?"

There were three soft knocks on his wall. Then two more. The same code Jessie had used as a kid to check if he was awake. Jared held his breath. Knocked back. Two—pause—three. He used his blanket to wipe the sweat from his forehead, then pushed it aside.

Jessie was sitting up in bed, blanket pulled to her chin. Jared knelt at her side, but she lifted the blanket.

"Get in," she said.

As a kid she would lie in bed with Jared and they would talk all night. It had been a long time since then. Jared slid in next to her, felt her legs press against his.

"Brr," she said, and laughed. "So, did you like her?"

"I don't know," Jared said. "She was nice."

"Nice, huh?"

"I guess."

Jessie's hand ran down Jared's arm, tangled into the knot of his clasped fingers. She reclined, so he was hovering above her.

"Did you kill anyone?"

Jared nodded.

"It was your job, though."

He nodded again.

"Remember after I saw you with Olivia?" Jessie pulled Jared's hand, ran it up her side, under her shirt. "You said one day I'd have tits, too." She mashed his hand against her chest, the skin cool against his fingers which had been warmed by Jessie's body.

It's just a touch.

"Now I do," Jessie said, beginning to massage his hands into her breasts. She was pressing her body hard into his. She reached under the blanket, into his boxers and held his penis tight. "You told me what goes where."

Jared remembered. He remembered saying it in a way not unlike the way he'd been told, even though he hadn't wanted Mr. Kansky's words coming from his mouth. He never wanted those words, not in Mr. Kansky's whisper lingering in his thoughts, and certainly not coming from his own mouth.

"Yes," Jared said. He needed a glass of water. Another desert feeling blurring his reality. He was above Jessie now, both of them tugging at each other's clothes and flesh. He closed his eyes tighter and pushed, told himself it had not been time to come home. That it never would.

WEST

When Stephen Linkfelt was headed to his locker to retrieve his father's M14 semi-automatic rifle, Cal Jones was in Art History getting ready to ask if he could visit the restroom. It was game day and as such Cal, West High's three-year starting Quarterback was dressed in slacks, dress shirt, tie, and jersey. But that wasn't the only game-day tradition Cal observed.

The season opener had been a disaster. A 56-7 romp courtesy of Colony. For the first time in his high school career the competition for state was wide open and Cal had big dreams. Dreams of playing college football in the Lower 48. He wasn't dreaming too big, of course. He believed in being practical. He didn't imagine himself at USC or Ohio State. But Boise State was a possibility, or maybe, if he had a great season, University of Oregon. But after that first week doubt set in and when the second game was on the horizon he was getting nervous.

It was midday, Economics, when his girlfriend, Jeannie Foster, passed him a note saying to meet her in the girls bathroom. Jeannie, a good girlfriend accustomed to the emotional acuity of her boyfriend, had sensed Cal's nervous energy and took it upon herself to ease his tension. So Cal met Jeannie and they fucked against the wall of the handicap stall.

That night West beat Eagle River 48-21, behind Cal's three passing touchdowns. He'd even run for one. Thus Cal developed another game day ritual, equally as important as eating a meal of Captain Crunch, two scrambled eggs, and two pieces of toast with strawberry jam.

X X X

Miles Linkfelt, Stephen's younger brother by a year and eight months, was in Biology when he got Stephen's text message. It said, GO TO THE PARKING LOT. While Miles and Stephen didn't exactly get along, they didn't not get along either. He held his phone under the desk and texted back, WHAT'S UP? But there was no answer.

x x x

Stephanie Frank was West High's new English teacher. She had moved to Anchorage from Montana, figuring it couldn't be all that different. Beside, her fiancee was working on a construction crew on the North Slope where he was gone for four to six weeks at a time. At least being in Anchorage they would be in the same state as one another.

When she passed Stephen Linkfelt—a student in her fourth period Shakespeare class—in the hall as she headed to the teacher's lounge, she noticed sweat dripping from the boy's forehead as he fiddled with the combination of his locker. "Everything all right?" she asked, continuing to walk toward the stairs at the end of the hall.

Stephen chuckled, the same nervous gurgle of a laugh that exited his mouth when she called on him to read aloud in class. "I always spin past the second number," he said.

"Have a good weekend," Stephanie said as she started down the stairs, and, as an afterthought, "Go Eagles."

"Go Eagles."

Stephen's voice followed her down the steps, as did the click of his locker finally opening.

x x x

Jeannie Foster was staring at herself in the girls room mirror. Fluffing her hair, adjusting her bra, smelling her armpits. Her boyfriend, Cal, would be walking through the door any minute. She chewed her spearmint gum vigorously for ten more seconds. She counted them out in her head, then spat it into the trash.

The hair on her arms stood up and her legs shook a little. It was, after all, a public bathroom. They were lucky to have not been caught yet and were tempting fate by continuing the practice. But if Cal was consistent about one thing it was his game-day routines. Especially when the team was winning. And because Jeannie loved her boyfriend she smiled at herself in the mirror then slipped her panties off from under her skirt, to make things a little quicker, and tucked them into her backpack.

x x x

Cal took a breath mint from his pocket and looked at his watch. He'd give it a minute to dissolve before asking to use the bathroom. At the same moment Stephen was wiping sweat from his forehead with his sleeve, then finally steadying his nerves long enough to open his locker.

Miles checked his cell phone for the third time, still finding no reply from his brother. Maybe there's going to be a fire drill, Miles thought and texted, FR DRL? to Stephen, while holding his phone inside the pocket of his cargo pants. Stephen was friendly with several teachers at West High and always seemed to have insider information on things like fire drills or changes in the lunch menu.

Mr. Lyle, the Biology teacher was diagramming what the class would be looking for when it came time to dissect their frogs. Miles stared into the drawing of a frog cut in half, wondered how he would bring himself to stick a knife into the rubbery hide of the amphibian.

"It's not so bad," Stephen had told him. "Though you can always be the inevitable wuss to plead his way out of it in exchange for dissecting a flower."

Miles and Stephen had caught frogs as kids. Baxter Bog was right outside their backyard fence and the two boys were constantly unlatching the gate and slipping out onto the gravel path when their parents were busy making dinner or paying bills. Miles thought about the slippery frog skin in his hands, holding them tight so they didn't jump free until he was ready to let them go. It wouldn't be so bad to have people think he was a wuss.

x x x

Stephanie sat at the formica table in the teacher's lounge, blowing on her Cup O' Soup. The Spanish teacher, Señorita Whitefield was the only other teacher in the lounge. Stephanie took a folded piece of paper from her pocket, laid it on the table next to her soup. It was a note from Principal Holsworth, asking her to dinner.

Stephanie thought about her husband, who had been away for three weeks during his current stint at work, and still had three to go. It was a long time for anyone to be away from their spouse, but Stephanie had an easier time with it when they were first married. When she still lived in a place where she had family and friends. She was happy to move anywhere to be nearer to her husband, but she was starting to think he'd been wrong when he said they would be closer to one another if she lived in Alaska.

"Dinner? My house, after the football game?" the note said. Principal Holsworth was only recently divorced, but Stephanie remembered the way his eyes were glued to her chest when she interviewed for the job. At the time she thought, if it helps me get the job, what the hell. And Holsworth wasn't so bad looking. He was a little older of a man than she saw herself with, but after a few weeks without her husband in bed next to her, Stephanie thought maybe settling a bit wasn't such a bad thing.

x x x

The door to the girls room opened and Jeannie held her breath. But it wasn't Cal. Just some girl Jeannie didn't recognize. Probably a freshman. The fact that the girl wouldn't even look at Jeannie made that probably a definite. Jeannie basked in the glow of the upperclassman intimidation factor. The girl went into the stall next to the handicap one and Jeannie tapped her foot, hoped it would be quick.

She turned on the faucet and washed her hands. For the hell of it. She checked her cell phone. Again. Cal was one minute late. Knowing him, it would be another five before he showed up. Jeannie hoped that this time, at least, he'd remembered to suck on a breath mint. The last time it had been taco day at lunch and his breath had smelled of cafeteria guacamole.

Jeannie kept the water on until she heard the toilet flush. She didn't want to hear the freshman pee. When the girl exited the stall she came to the sink and washed her hands without looking up. She didn't even check herself in the mirror. Jeannie looked her up and down. The girl wasn't so much of a mess, but she was still a freshman.

x x x

Cal raised his hand. "Can I use the bathroom?" The team's tight end snickered behind him because he knew Cal's routine. Ms. Rodriquez waved Cal toward the door. Cal patted his pocket, to make sure he had a condom, felt its tell-tale outline under the denim, and rose from his desk. He was already getting hard.

When Cal opened room 215's door, Stephen was at the end of the hall, maybe half the length of a football field in the direction Cal was headed, loading a round of ammunition into his father's gun. When Cal noticed Stephen, the door was just clicking shut behind him.

x x x

Miles looked into the tin dish where his frog lay lifeless and slick under the slight flicker of the florescent lights. He wondered how Stephen could have cut into one. After all, Stephen had enjoyed the frog-catching even more than Miles. He had kept one as a pet for two months. Secret from their parents. And when it died Stephen cried for two days. Sure, they were nine and seven-and-a-half back then, but still.

Mr. Lyle made eye contact with Miles and mimed a cutting motion. Miles held the scalpel at a forty-five degree angle, poised just above the frog's white speckled stomach. He lowered his hand until the blade rested on the frog's skin, creating a small dimple.

There was a loud echoing blast in the hallway. Miles' hand slipped and the scalpel skated across the frog's stomach and sliced into its throat. Liquid oozed into the dish and Miles dropped the blade.

x x x

Stephanie texted her husband, HOW'S WORK? LUV U! even though she knew at this point in the day he was probably fighting against permafrost to dig a trench where electricians would run wires. And his cell phone was probably back in his room at the camp. But she was feeling guilty for considering Principal Holsworth's invitation. Feeling guilty for leaning toward accepting.

She tried to distract herself as she ate her soup. Thought about the boy in the hall, Stephen Linkfelt. He did well in her Shakespeare class, especially given his nervousness when reading aloud. He seemed to get along with his classmates, but there was something off about him, too. Maybe, she thought, he was just awkward around her because he had a crush. She had, after all, noticed him staring at her during reading time in class. Or getting lost in her cleavage when she tried to talk to him about late homework last week.

For a second she wondered what he looked like naked. He was a senior and seemed in good shape. Why didn't he play sports? She ate a spoonful of soup, careful not to slurp because Señorita Whitefield was still in the lounge. She thought about the sweat dripping down Stephen's forehead when she passed him. That's what it would look like, she thought, during a strenuous fuck. She flipped Principal Holsworth's note in her fingers. She was getting herself excited, her thighs tingling. There was a loud noise upstairs, a clash and echo, as she made up her mind to have dinner with the principal.

x x x

Jeannie was growing impatient. She looked at the time again. If Cal was more than five minutes late her panties were going back on and she was returning to study hall. Screw his game day superstitions.

She was fluffing her hair and pouting her lips in the mirror for the hundredth time when the crack rang out like thunder in the hall. She went queasy. Her father had taken her hunting since she was a little girl. She knew the sound of a gun. She opened the bathroom door and looked out. Someone was standing by the lockers holding an M14. She knew the kid from something. Her Shakespeare class. Stephen.

Jeannie froze in the doorway. He hadn't noticed her yet, and though she knew she should retreat, hide herself in the stall where she'd expected to be having sex with her boyfriend right about now, she couldn't move.

Stephen began walking down the hallway. Jeannie took a step out of the bathroom, the door swinging closed behind her. When it latched shut, she cringed. Stephen turned, looked her in the eye. He was always looking at her in class, she realized now, like she was feeling a stare for the first time. Out of habit Jeannie raised a hand to cover her cleavage. Stephen, in turn, raised the gun.

Stephen Linkfelt was not angry. He wasn't mixed up, or feeling left out. He was not an outcast, as seemed to be the stereotype for what he had been planning. He couldn't fully explain it, but could, if nothing else, pinpoint the initial thought to the day he first held his father's M14. His dad, an engineer for BP, was an avid weapons collector, had multiple lockers in the garage and basement full of guns, knives, and even swords.

Even though he knew how he would come to be characterized by the media, and the sound-bytes of friends, family, classmates, teachers, and neighbors, he thought the plan was worth it. It came down to one thing: mediocrity.

Stephen knew he was no genius, he wasn't particularly skilled in any area, skating by with high Cs and low Bs his entire academic career. He wasn't athletically gifted, either, erring more on clumsy. And mediocrity only resulted in one thing in Alaska: working a mediocre job for the rest of your life. He was primed to end up working on a construction crew on the North Slope, on a fishing boat, or in a hatchery.

Aching deep within him, Stephen had always wanted to be famous, but mediocrity did not result in fame. Ever. People got famous for being great, or for being horrible at something, like the folks who auditioned for shows like American Idol and got famous for singing off-time, out of tune, and with a slur. Those people sometimes got more famous than the people who were great at something.

But Stephen wasn't even horrible at anything. He was just middle of the road, average.

Sure, he experienced nerves when the day came. He could barely open his damn locker his heart was pounding so fast, and his hands were so sweaty. Seeing that new English teacher, Mrs. Frank didn't help, either. She was wearing a tight sweater and her breasts —all breasts—made him nervous. Like he couldn't control his insides from revolting against him when a girl was around.

But he was going to be good at this one thing. He was determined. So he took a deep breath, put Mrs. Frank out of his mind, and opened the locker.

The gun was cold in his hands. He gripped and re-gripped, pitting it against his shoulder. He loaded a round of ammunition. Down the hall a door opened.

Cal Jones, the quarterback, stepped out and looked right at Stephen. This was the moment, the true test.

Stephen took a deep breath as Cal stared down the hall at him. He slid his finger along the trigger, pulled.

Cal fell to the ground like he'd been sacked by an invisible middle linebacker. The blood in Stephen's veins ran hot. He wiped sweat from his eyes. There was a click of a door behind him and he turned to find Jeannie, Cal's girlfriend, walking out of the bathroom.

For a second Stephen thought of sparing her. He'd had a crush on her since fifth grade, though it was unlikely she even knew his name. He looked at her tanning-salon brown legs, her hand placed modestly over her chest. He imagined her so grateful that she got naked for him. But he knew there would be no time for that, not with what would happen to him after today. He lifted the gun from his side, lined up the sight with the divot of her cleavage.

x x x

When Stephen pushed open the door to the biology lab the first person he saw was his brother, Miles. He had texted Miles to go to the damn parking lot. "Fuck," he said, and razed the room. There was no turning back at this point. He'd made it through the second floor, and was surprised the police had yet to arrive. Of course it was only a matter of time.

Stephen ran down the stairs at the end of the hall. He had been sure he'd have been stopped by this point. There was one thing left he wanted to do. Not for fame or infamy, but for himself. And since he'd yet to hear a siren, he headed for the teacher's lounge.

He walked past classrooms he knew were full of students. But this was not about revenge against certain people as the media would surely portray it. There was no desire to kill a certain number of people, only to make a mark. So, the students and teachers on the first floor would survive to talk about the high school massacre in Anchorage to news crews and national morning shows.

Stephen swung open the door to the teacher's lounge and found Mrs. Frank huddled on the couch at the back of the room with the Spanish teacher, Señorita Whitefield. He soaked in the surprise and horror on their faces before pointing the gun at Señorita Whitefield. "Over there," he said, sweeping the gun to point at the corner, near the refrigerator. "Por favor," he added, pleased with his improvisation. When she had relocated he squeezed the trigger, and she dropped to the ground.

Mrs. Frank was crying uncontrollably, but in her silent gasps for air between sobs, Stephen heard sirens finally approaching. There was no point, he knew, in playing the nice guy. He lifted the gun, pointed it at her chest, knowing full well the round was empty. "Get undressed," he said.

Mrs. Frank shakily removed her shirt and undid her bra, her breasts dropping with a heft that surprised Stephen. He dropped his father's gun and reached out, touched Mrs. Frank's chest. He could feel her heart pounding wildly, feel her body trembling, the sweat beading from her pores. He thought he heard a helicopter circling above the school.

Stephen reached into his belt and pulled out another gun, a 9mm. Mrs. Frank unbuttoned her pants, hands quaking like she hadn't eaten in days. Stephen shook his head, closed his eyes, lifted the gun.

The sirens were right outside now, the parking lot filled with police cars. This is it, Stephen thought, placing the barrel to the side of his head. This is forever. Go Eagles.

THE BATHROOM WALL

The bathroom wall has a funny texture about it. When I stare at it pictures begin to emerge. Lions with sunglasses, old men in funny hats, melting palm trees. It's never the same thing twice, even when I go searching for one I've already seen. I get lost in the game of it when I'm sitting on the toilet, drying off after a shower, or when I should be brushing my teeth.

Sometimes Dad yells for me, and I realize I've been standing with my toothbrush in my mouth for a couple minutes. The pictures scramble away. The wall goes back to just being a wall. Sometimes Dad comes and cuffs me in the back of the head and knocks the toothbrush right out from between my teeth.

Sometimes I see our dog Goose in the wall. He died last fall, got lost in a snowstorm and couldn't find his way home. When the snow stopped we found his body buried in a snowdrift between the road and the woods. Goose was frozen solid, looked like a statue.

Dad drank more than usual that night. He yelled at me for letting Goose out. And I didn't say a thing when he hit me, even though it was Dad who left Goose in the bed of the truck in the parking lot at the liquor store, didn't have him tied up or nothing. Dad told me I needed to learn some responsibility. That I spend too much time daydreaming. He pulled me onto his lap and spanked me with his hand. Then his belt.

I didn't sit on the toilet that night, but I brushed my teeth for a long time and even flossed twice.

"Crap or get off the pot," Dad yelled from the kitchen.

Fact is I've never seen Dad in that wall. The harder I look the less I see of him, or his knee, or the belt coming down behind me. I keep staring at the wall, like the pictures are a puzzle or code, figuring if I look hard enough I'll find a way out.

LIKE SWIMMING

"How's your brain?" Joe asks.

The doctors fucked up the operation. All Jaws wanted was the tumor gone, but now he's lacking short term memory as well.

"All good on the northern front," he says, tapping the side of his head. He gets the question every day and is running out of ways to pretend everything is fine.

Like a secret to-do list, Jaws writes his tasks in a small notebook and keeps it in his shirt pocket. When no one is looking he pulls it out and reminds himself of what he's supposed to be doing. Carrying three two-by-sixteen planks of lumber on his shoulder, he stops. Hunching over, he rests the wood on the ground.

"That's right," he says to himself, "the wood is going to the electrician's shack."

He hoists the load again and finishes the delivery. Each job takes at least one of these pit stops. Once, in the middle of cutting iron bolts with a Metabo, he had to stop after a handful to remind himself there were still a dozen left.

Construction in the Arctic is probably the worst and deadliest thing he could be doing in his condition. And he poses as much danger, if not more, to his coworkers as he does to himself. But he's been doing this work for ten years—since graduating high school, and it's all he knows.

Keeping up is becoming a job in itself. Just remembering everybody is a chore. Jaws keeps a cheat sheet of their names and characteristics. It's the first page in the notebook. Joe: crew foreman, bad teeth, red hair and beard.

"Jesus," Joe says, walking next to Jaws as they leave the break shack. "You'd think the top of the world would get a little warmer in the middle of Ju-ly."

Jaws laughs, and it feels like old times for a fleeting second before he has to check for Red Beard's name.

"Twenty-two ain't bad. At least it's sunny. Before you know it we'll be back in the negatives."

Joe nods and Jaws thanks God some things have stuck with him, the vernacular and blue collar lilt. It's as if they were engrained. Genetic even.

And at least everything he knew before is intact. It's just new things he can't retain. Sometimes something sticks for thirty minutes, but more often it's half that. After ten years of the same job, same company, Jaws can't believe his shit luck being sent to a crew where he didn't know a soul. His regular crew is at North Star, but they were full up and he was needed at Pump Station 1.

Over the years he'd done a lot of jobs at P.S. 1. Flying into Deadhorse and bunking at M.C.C. felt as close to home as anything.

"Take a ride with me," Joe says, pulling himself into one of the company pickups.

"Sure," Jaws says.

He buckles the seatbelt and is thankful most of the basic safety regulations haven't changed in years. If they do he'll have them tattooed. Like in that movie, Memento people were raving about a few years ago.

"We've got a new guy flying in tomorrow," Joe says. "I want you to pick him up from the airport, show him the ropes around here."

"First timer?"

"Yep. Nineteen. Dad works on a crew at Pump Station 5."

"Whose kid?"

"Rob Landry. Ever worked with him?"

Jaws chews his lip.

"Once or twice. Think we bunked together at Kuparuk a few years back."

If there were an entry for Landry it would read, master carpenter, no sense of humor.

"Well you're my man. After the toolbox meeting in the morning take truck nine and pick him up."

Jaws hunches toward the door of the truck and writes it in the notebook. They pass under the vapor flare, louder than usual in the afternoon's high wind. The sound is like a jet on the tarmac. For a moment the roar relieves him of thought, of remembering a goddamn thing. But the truck stops and Joe says, "Here you are."

"Thanks," Jaws says and steps out on the pad.

He's facing the carpentry shack and drawing a blank. He waits for the truck to pull away before checking the notebook. Take six barricades to new trench, west side of pad.

He loads the barricades into the back of a Kubota and drives them across the pump station. He knows the place the way other people know their neighborhoods. He stops at the nine-hole for a piss, then makes it to the unfinished trench running parallel to the holding tanks reading Gas #1 and Gas #2.

The Mud Dog team is still sucking dirt out of the hole when he unloads the Kubota. Dave: brown hair, beard, glass eye cuts off the Dog's power and taps Jesse (blonde, goatee) on the shoulder.

"Thanks, man." Dave says.

"No prob."

In tandem Dave and Jesse remove their hard hats and wipe their foreheads. Jaws remembers seeing this sort of synchronicity in Mud Dog teams before. Like the bond between twins.

"Any ground water problems with this one?" Jaws asks, pointing at the trench. At twenty feet long the thing is only half done.

"Not as bad as one-o-seven," Jesse says, motioning between the holding tanks. "That one keeps filling up like a damn swimming pool."

"How many sumps you running?"

"Two," Jesse says, and Dave adds, "One at each end."

"Just not keeping up, huh?"

Dave shakes his head. "We're going to wait until the sparkies are ready to lay cable, then we'll pull the hose over there and suck the water with the truck. Keep it dry while they do their thing, then we'll refill her and compact the sucker as fast as we can."

Jaws knows the drill, but guys on the slope are always more than eager to explain what they're doing. It passes the time, breaks the monotony. He looks down into the four-foot deep hole. Not so different from a grave, he thinks. Only two feet away. Suddenly everything gets dark and his feet give way.

Dave reaches out, pulls Jaws back from the edge of the trench, holds onto him until his legs have resettled.

"You all right?"

"Just lost my footing."

Jaws keeps his eyes on the ground until he climbs back into the Kubota. He can't afford such close calls.

The doctors warned him not to go back to work. No way to know how the brain will react, they said. But if he'd delayed his return that would have meant telling the company what had happened.

Dave and Jesse have the Mud Dog running again and Jaws waves as he drives away, hoping they won't say anything to Joe.

Quitting time has never changed. Six in the morning to six at night—that's always been Jaws' shift. Seven days a week. Six weeks at a time. So when Jaws checks his watch and it says 5:30, there's no reminder needed that it's time to head back to the break shack and get on the bus to M.C.C. He stuffs his gloves, safety vest and glasses into his hard hat as he walks. There's a corner of the bench at the second plastic table where he places them at the end of every day. Another left-over ritual.

Jaws gets on the bus and stares out the window at the melted tundra, all standing puddles. Soon enough, though, it will turn back to ice and be covered with snow.

Having less to remember has made it easier for Jaws to fall asleep. But the dreams are more vivid now. Tonight he dreams he's at a hotel with a nice pool in the center of the building. No one else seems to be staying at the place. Jaws is facing the pool. He's wearing jeans and a t-shirt. And new tennis shoes, which only stand out because he's so used to wearing his Xtra Tuff boots at work. By the time his two weeks of R&R end he's barely gotten used to real shoes.

The next thing Jaws knows he's in the pool. Fully clothed, and completely submersed. He's floating there, eyes open, taking in the hotel's Greco-Roman decor from under the water, lending the world a bluish tint. He begins talking to himself, but it's all gurgles and bubbles that rise to the surface and pop silently, rippling the surface.

Just as he's starting to disappear in the water his alarm clock starts beeping. 4 a.m. Jaws sits up. It's the first time he's been in a single room—his one lucky break—and he hasn't gotten used to not having to worry about a roommate's schedule. He writes his room number on his hand, grabs his toothbrush, and walks down the hall in his boxers to the community bathroom.

Back in his room he gets dressed. The routine has changed little since his first time on the slope. Two pairs of socks, a tank top, a long sleeve shirt, Carhartt jeans, and a hooded sweatshirt. For colder days he has a Carhartt jacket. And long underwear. Next he goes to the cafeteria. Breakfast is scrambled eggs, four pieces of bacon, two sausage links, hash browns, and a glass of orange juice.

The bus ride to the pump station in the mornings always seems shorter than the ride back to camp at night. Dave and Jesse are in the seat in front of him.

"That noggin's been through a lot," Dave says, looking back at Jaws.

"I wish people would stop talking about my head," Jaws says and immediately regrets it.

"You ever get used to it?" Jesse asks. "Life as a sloper, I mean."

On the one hand, Jaws has been used to his life for a long time. But the question comes at an awkward time; he doesn't feel used to anything anymore.

"I did," he says. "But I've seen a lot of people come and go who could never get the hang of it. It's a different life, but you can get accustomed to it if you want."

"I guess so. I've been doing it two years, but everyday I think about going back to being broke, making furniture."

"It's like swimming," Jaws says, remembering his dream from the night before. "Just 'cause you know how doesn't mean you can't drown."

Jesse gives Jaws a funny look.

"Just because you know what you're doing up here, in terms of the job, doesn't mean you can't get overwhelmed. A lot of people come thinking it's just another construction gig. They get burned out. If you come into it accepting it for what it is, you're likelier to survive."

"That's deep," Dave says.

The bus stops outside the pump station gates and a security guard boards the bus to check everyone's ID badges. Out the window a few caribou are grazing. It's a sight Jaws never tires of, every year he looks forward to August when the herds migrate in the hundreds across the tundra.

Once on the pump station pad the bus drops the electricians at their break shack, then the construction crew at theirs. The toolbox meeting addresses the proper care and storage of tools. There are only so many possible topics, so they get rotated regularly. After that it's hard hats on and out to work. For Jaws that means getting in a truck and going back in the direction of M.C.C., to the Deadhorse airport.

The drive takes about thirty minutes, but the plane is late. So Jaws spends his morning waiting in the airport, which is about the size of a small restaurant. When the plane does land about twenty guys get off and crowd around the area where their luggage will be tossed.

Only one person looks younger than Jaws, so that's who he approaches.

"Landry?" he asks.

The kid turns, his cheeks are smooth. Probably doesn't even shave twice a month yet, Jaws thinks. At least when he made his first trip to the slope he had that. And by the time he left for his first R&R he'd grown a decent beard. Facial hair assimilation, he called it.

"John Ridge," he says, extending his hand. "But you can call me Jaws."

"Jason," the kids says and steps away to grab his bag from the metal tray bolted to the wall.

In the truck Jaws gives Jason safety glasses, tells him to put them on--slope rules.

"We'll stop and get your room at M.C.C. so you can drop off your bag, then we'll head out to the pump station."

"You a lifer like my dad?"

"Seem to be," Jaws says. "Started around your age. That your plan?"

"No, just trying to make some cash before I start college."

"What are you going to study?"

"Thinking about biology. But I'm not sure yet."

"You've got time."

Jaws wonders when that stops being true.

"So, what's in store for me?"

"Well, it sounds like you'll be getting the grab bag. I'll show you the ropes. I'm kind of a utility man. Carpentry, scaffolding, digging. Lots of digging."

"I dig," Jason says and laughs at his own joke.

At the pump station Jaws gets the kid outfitted with a hard hat, gloves, and a safety vest, then takes him on a tour of the pad. It's hard to check his notebook with somebody else around all the time, but Jaws has no choice.

"It's not much," Jaws says when they arrive back at the break shack. "But if you're not careful it'll start feeling like home."

"Sounds like my dad. Once, in middle school, I figured out he spent seventy-five percent of his time up here."

"I believe it."

"Doesn't leave much time for anything else, does it?"

"Working here either becomes your life, or you move onto something else. But it's hard to walk away from the money. I can only imagine it's harder when you have a family."

"You going to do this for the rest of your life?"

For the first time since his diagnosis Jaws is thankful. Of course all the heartbreak is still there. All the relationships that couldn't weather the life of working on the slope. But there's no longer the pressure to try. He can't imagine chasing a woman or keeping one. And for once it has nothing to do with his job.

"Jaws," Jason says, and he's at looking Jaws like it might have been the fourth or fifth time he's said it.

"Yeah?"

"You going to work up here forever?"

"I'll do it as long as I can," he says. "As long as they'll let me."

He realizes how pathetic he must sound to a kid getting ready to go to college. And now he's stuck with a picture of himself as one of the old-timers who's only kept around to sweep out the break shacks, an existence he could have never fathomed a few weeks ago.

"It's what I know, what I'm good at." Jaws can't wait to forget this conversation. He looks at Jason fiddling with his hard hat and tries to imagine a time when things like hard hats didn't feel comfortable. He wasn't so different from Jason at one time, but he knows that thought is wrong, romanticized. He knew from his first day this would be his career.

Jaws scales a tower of scaffolding and starts taking it apart, lowering the pieces down to Jason.

"Everything we do," he says, "will eventually be invisible. If we do our work right there will be no trace of how things got the way we leave them."

"Like the pyramids or something."

"Kind of, only we don't get any sort of monument." Jaws laughs.

From his perch he can see a good portion of the pump station. There are several open trenches waiting for the electricians to lay cable. The pipeline strikes across the tundra, Jaws tries to picture its whole path, crisscrossing the state. In the distance there's a vapor flare from one of many processing sites.

"You know," he says, "it's been ten years and this place looks pretty much the same."

Jason grabs the crossbeam Jaws is lowering. He's an intent worker already and pays attention to what he is being taught.

"I hope this is your only stay on the slope," Jaws says.

"I do, too."

"Get a degree, do something better with your life."

Jason nods, sets down the crossbeam, readies himself for the next.

I can't keep this up, Jaws thinks. It's been hard enough and it's only been a couple weeks. He certainly can't survive another decade. And training somebody else? It's too much. He lowers another piece of scaffold and looks at his notebook.

"Jason," he says, "in an hour I'm not going to remember any of this."

Jason lifts his hard hat, shields his eyes from the sun.

"I had an operation."

"Holy shit. Serious?"

"If anybody finds out about it I'm out of a job. I'm out of a life."

Jason is still holding the last crossbeam. It's at his side like a walking stick.

"I won't rat you out."

"I can't keep looking at a notebook every fifteen minutes for the rest of my life. But what am I going to do if I'm not doing this? Drink and sleep?"

The dirt is moving, shifting, changing color. It's no longer gray and brown, it's all blue. It's becoming water and the ripples are washing right over the kid's head.

"I want to swim," Jaws says. His head is cloudy, like when the anesthetic took hold.

"What?"

Jason lets the crossbeam fall to the ground and starts climbing the metal bars.

"Hold on, Jaws."

The kid reaches the top and grabs Jaws by the shoulder.

"It's just like the pool," Jaws says.

"I don't know what you're talking about."

Jaws can barely feel the kid's grip. He hangs onto the one crossbeam he hasn't disassembled on the top level of the tower and waits for the bluish glaze to disappear. The pump station, too. The trenches, holding tanks, pickups, and break shacks. Even the pipeline. He holds on until it's just him, the tundra, and the migrating herds of caribou heading to a place where there is no short or long term, only a now.

TRENCH SWIMMER

The vapor flare cracks like a bull whip. And the steady static makes it sound like I'm under a jumbo jet instead of on a pump station pad in the arctic. The Mud Dog is my truck. Says FIDO on the driver's side door. I'm dressed in rain gear, the rubber pants swishing between my thighs. Water's building up in the north trench and there's nothing I can do about it.

Danny lumbers back from the nine-hole, a set of port-a-potties enclosed in a shack. We stare over the edge. The trench was twenty-six inches across and four feet deep when we dug it. Now the sides are caving in and the bottom is silting. The electricians won't be able to lay cable at this rate.

The twelve-volt water pump is on the fritz again, and we're both plumb out of ideas. I grab a bucket out of Fido's side hatch and toss it to Danny, still looking at his two-day stubble in the ground water reflection.

"You know what to do," I say over the whip of the flare.

Back at Danny's side I kneel down and peel off my left boot. A hundred dollars down the trench, I think and dip it into the rising water. We frantically dish the water out of the hole, cussing the damn sparkies and their cable.

"I got a cable I'll lay for 'em," Danny says.

When we get back to camp tonight I'll borrow a company truck and head into the general store in Deadhorse. Buy myself a new pair of boots. Other than that it'll be the same thing tomorrow. Wake up at four, on the bus at five, to the pump station by six. Danny and I'll be driving the Mud Dog, sucking dirt and permafrost to make way for cables, all so we can fill it back in when the electricians are done.

I've heard about guys getting cabin fever. The slope's its own sort of isolation. I've got nothing to go home to since my girlfriend dumped me, so I've been stretching my stints. It's been eight weeks straight this time. Twelve hours a day, seven days a week.

"Dare you to swim it," I say, not thinking about the words that are coming out of my mouth.

"You losing it?" Danny looks at me, slack-jawed like a steelhead that's just been pulled out of the water.

"Just trying to break the monotony." Suddenly I'm overwhelmed by the sheer routine of the job. My brain feels like it's operating on an hour of sleep, half-speed and fogged over.

"You want to break the monotony so bad, why don't you swim it?"

Before he can start his half-chuckle half-smoker's cough, I'm peeling off my other boot and throwing off the rain gear.

"You have lost it," Danny says, standing up from the edge of the trench.

I don't say a word, just keep stripping until I'm in my gray long underwear and shivering uncontrollably. I put my hands together over my head like a swimmer you'd see in the Olympics or something and dive in. When I hit the water my brain suddenly wakes up, moves from slow motion to fast forward, thoughts rushing so fast I can't grasp them all.

I'll probably lose my job. And be known as the trench swimmer. I will become a tall tale. Guys doing this work for years to come will tell the story, each year making it a little bigger, a little more spectacular. They'll use the story to forget about digging trenches twelve hours a day.

I close my eyes against the silt and mud. My skin, my insides, feel like layers of permafrost. It's worth it, I think, wondering how long I can stay under before I'll have to rise to the surface for air.

MORNING FOR NIGHT

"It's like he's been gone forever," the woman at the end says.

Crocker turns on his stool. "The slope?"

"Prison," she says, shrugging her bony shoulders and forcing a smile.

"Oh." Crocker turns back to his Jack and Coke, stirring it with a quick whirl of the straw before taking a sip. "Sorry about that. Just, you know, guys on the slope are gone six, eight weeks at a time."

The woman stands, Crocker watches her hair fall across her face in curls of brown and gray. She takes the stool next to him.

"I'm Jill," she says.

"Crocker."

"You work on the slope, huh?"

He nods. "Just to warn you, we're not known for being good company."

"You'll do fine."

"Here's to that." Crocker tips his glass in Jill's direction.

"What do you do up there?"

"Foreman. That your husband? In prison?"

She takes a drink. "Yeah."

"Rough," Crocker says, watches her in the mirror behind the rows of liquor bottles. Her lips, thin reeds, tighten. "What landed him there?"

"Killed a guy in a fight." She raises an eyebrow, waiting for Crocker to react.

"I've worked with a lot of ex-cons." Crocker runs a napkin over the oak, wiping away the ring of condensation under his glass. "They're not all bad."

"Nick's never been good when he drinks." Jill shakes her head. "But I never thought he could do something like that."

Crocker takes the last swallow of his drink. "Sorry. I've lost some hard workers to that shit."

"Yeah," she says, getting quiet and twisting her glass in circles.

"How long?"

"Seven months." She sighs, tucks her hair behind her ear. "Just sixteen to eighteen more years to go."

"Long time, no two ways about it."

"So," Jill says, pushing out a laugh, "how do we save the evening now?"

The bartender slides another Jack and Coke in front of Crocker. "There's nothing to save," he says. "Nothing's been ruined." He points at her glass and she nods. As Crocker waves for a refill his cell phone beeps. "Oops," he says and pulls the phone from his jean pocket.

"Girlfriend?"

"Daughter," Crocker says, chuckling. "She sends me these text messages all the time."

"How old?"

"Eighteen. First year of college in Arizona."

"And her mom?"

Crocker shows his empty ring finger. "No wife."

"Where's she?"

He shrugs and claps his phone shut on his thigh. "You got kids?"

"Nick never wanted any."

"Did you?"

"There was a time, I guess, where I thought about it." Jill's drink arrives and she takes a sip. "Did you work on the slope when your daughter was a kid?"

"Made a few trips. Mostly I worked local sites until she left. Didn't want Lizzie to be alone."

"You raised her by yourself?"

Crocker nods, takes a long drink.

Jill stands, excuses herself. The powder room she called it. Better than the "hole," like on work sites. Normally Crocker would tell a person not to fall in, instead he says, "I'll be right here" and watches her disappear down the hallway past the bar.

He scrapes at the dirt beneath his fingernails with the tip of his pocketknife. The bar is nearly empty. There's one couple in the back corner, cozying up to one another in front of the small fireplace. The thick, warm musk of burning pine logs fogs the room. There were a couple guys in suits earlier--the price of being in Anchorage, but they've left. Crocker is tapping his foot, even though there's no music. He puts a hand on his knee, steadying his nerves and the shaking stool. He felt the same sense of unease raising Lizzie, as if one mistake, one wrong move, would screw her up for life.

"Lost?" Jill asks, clicking her tongue and pretending to tap her fist on Crocker's head.

Crocker cleans the knife on his jeans, slides it back into his pocket. "Guess I was."

"I'm glad I came out tonight," Jill says. "This is more fun than I've had in a long time."

"That's sad," Crocker says, not hiding a smile.

Jill laughs, raises her glass to Crocker and he clinks his against it. "I don't think it should stop." She slides her hand along his shoulder.

"Want to dance?" Crocker asks, standing.

"I think you ought to come home with me."

Crocker eyes her over the rim of his glass, sets it back on the bar. "You're married," he says, and it's less than a whisper, but he knows she heard. He coughs into his hand, walks over to the jukebox and presses B-9 for Johnny Cash's "Orange Blossom Special." He extends a hand to Jill. "My father always said this was the only song worth dancing to," he says, pulling her close. Her perfume is sweet, like honey and fireweed. Crocker doesn't care they aren't moving in time with the music.

Jill takes his face in her hand, her fingertips rubbing against the stubble of his cheek. "I love my husband," she says. "But he's not here. Won't be for too long." She takes her hand away, places it on Crocker's back. "I don't want to go home alone, sleep alone, like every other night."

Crocker nods, keeps swaying to the song, which has been over for a good thirty seconds. Lizzie reminds him every time they talk that it's time he live for himself. "Let's see how it goes," he says.

Jill loops his hand around her hip, leads him back to the bar.

"Another round?" the bartender asks.

"Please," Crocker says.

Crocker finishes the last of the drink that's been melting while they danced and watches the bartender pour whiskey into two fresh glasses. Jill puts her hand on his knee, gives a light squeeze.

"What's it like, working up there?" she asks.

"Like another planet. Dark all winter, light all summer."

"Must be strange."

"You get used to it. Everything becomes routine."

The bartender sets the drinks in front of them and Crocker hands him a hundred dollar bill. "Keep the change," he says, and the bartender nods a thank you before turning to the register.

"Sounds kind of dreary, if you ask me," Jill says.

"Keeps me in the Jack Daniels." Crocker winks. "Makes it easy to send Lizzie to school."

"You're a good man."

Crocker rubs the back of his neck. "Nothing special," he says.

"I haven't met a lot of guys who've raised a kid on their own, or that worries about making sure they go to college."

He shrugs, takes a drink, hoping the blood flow will recede from his cheeks. When Lizzie was seven he broke up with a girlfriend because she didn't like the woman. "She doesn't feel like a mom," Lizzie had said as he tucked her into bed. "She's got a good head on her shoulders," Crocker says.

Jill pats his hand. "Let's get out of here," she says, then empties her glass.

"Got to finish this drink." Crocker toasts the air with his glass. "You can only shuffle your feet so long," he'd told Lizzie when she was deciding on a college. They were walking by the inlet. He knew she felt obliged to stay in Alaska, go to UAA, for her old man. "Make this decision for yourself," he'd said.

It's after eleven and the sun is finally setting, the all-night twilight of an Anchorage summer stretching over the city. "Let's take a walk," Crocker says, dialing a cab company and requesting one be sent to Elderberry Park in thirty minutes. He puts his arm over Jill's shoulder, fitting her body into the nook of his armpit, as they walk down West 5th Avenue toward Cook Inlet.

"I thought we were going to my house," Jill says.

"Let's watch the sunset."

"Are you a romantic?" she asks, teasing.

"Something like that," he says.

In a few minutes they are at the small triangular park by the train tracks. Jill weaves her arms under Crocker's, pulls herself flush with his chest. She pushes herself onto her toes and kisses his neck and ear lobe. "I want you to myself."

"There's no one else around," Crocker says.

"You know what I mean. I want to curl up with you."

"How about this?" He takes her hand, leads her past the small playground with the curly slide—Lizzie's favorite slide in the city—to the bench overlooking the water.

"I was thinking more like a couch," she says, looking past him. "Or a bed."

"I don't know anything about you."

"There's time to learn."

Crocker kisses her forehead.

"Besides," she says, "you know what's important. Everything else is stuff. Like curtains, just hanging there."

"What do you do for a living?"

Jill sucks on her lower lip and holds Crocker's knee. "I'm a dental assistant. You know, hand the doctor floss, adjust the chair." She smiles, the edges of her mouth stiff, barely reaching upward. "It's a job."

Crocker puts his hand on her cheek and it's like touching one of the dolls Lizzie left behind. He still sits in her room sometimes, pretending she's there, still young enough to have a story read to her. "All right," he says, for no other reason but to break the silence.

The sun is as set as it's going to get, a faint dusk lingering over the horizon, like it will until morning. Crocker used to skip rocks across the inlet and tell Lizzie he was going to get one all the way to the sun.

"What happened with your wife?" Jill asks.

The water laps over the rocks a few feet from the train tracks. "We moved down to Seattle and she got hooked on meth. Lizzie was only a couple years old, so I took her and moved back here."

Jill plays with Crocker's fingers, resting on her waist, and nuzzles his shoulder. "Tell me more about the arctic."

"Just a place." Crocker pulls her snug. "Men building things, tearing things down. Bears and caribou running around." He points toward the water, glistening a deep orange sherbet from the sun. "That's the color of the foxes," he says.

"Sounds better than here after all."

"Probably would be without the work."

"That's true about everywhere, isn't it?"

For a second Crocker feels like he's sitting with Lizzie, tucking her in to tales of wildlife encounters. Her favorites were always the run-ins with foxes. She found it hilarious that the sour stench of one could be smelled from hundreds of yards away. Crocker would say, "and then I got a whiff of sour fox" and before he could get to the part where he actually saw the animal prancing in the snow Lizzie would be curled in a ball, giggling. He slips his hand into his pocket and clutches his cell phone.

"You still there?"

"Sorry," he says. "College girls don't want messages from their fathers in the middle of the night, do they?" Jill pats Crocker's hand and he laughs. "Of course they don't."

Jill smiles at him, runs her hand through her hair. "When's the taxi coming?"

Crocker turns his wrist. "Any minute."

"It's time to stop stalling." Jill rests a hand on Crocker's thigh and he avoids her look.

Meeting her eyes isn't going to help him make a decision. Or it will, but maybe not the right one. The water is almost completely still, and Crocker has the urge to toss something in. Just to cause a few ripples.

"Look," Jill says, laughing and shaking Crocker's leg. "We'll just snuggle."

"You're a hard animal to resist," he says, turning to face her, "being all beautiful like you are." Crocker's hand is on her face, and he's stroking her cheek with his thumb.

The taxi pulls up to the curb by the park entrance. "I wish I could show you a summer night in the arctic," he says. "It's like having morning for night. Makes you feel like you're always starting a new day." He waves to the cab driver, letting him know they're coming. "What do you think a one-night stand would feel like up there, with nothing to signify the slate being wiped clean?"

"You're thinking too much," Jill says, tugging at Crocker's arm. "Let's go."

The inlet shimmers in a sudden breeze. A phantom cell phone vibration twitches against his leg. Lizzie may be awake, but she's sure as hell not thinking about her dad if she is.

Crocker opens the back door of the taxi and watches Jill climb in, gets in after her, wondering how it will all play out in the morning. How the sunlight will move on their bodies, the tangle of sheets. Like the slope, he thinks, seeing the sun in the middle of the night, it doesn't feel right or wrong. You just get used to it.

Whenever Lizzie asked about her mother, why they had left her behind, Crocker would say, "Sometimes a thing just is. Sometimes you just have to appreciate the unexplainable." Then his daughter would nod, pull the blankets up under her chin, and burrow her head into the pillow.

His thigh is pressed firmly against Jill's. She leans over the front seat, her perfume no longer as potent, and whispers an address to the driver. Crocker watches the inlet out the window, imagines its surface, its wrinkles exposed as the sun rises and works its way back to the horizon. Each and every day.

THE CONVERGENCE
OF CONTACT

I got in the truck early this morning. Already ninety-six deliveries out of the way. I'm eating lunch in the park again. It's 11:22, so there aren't many people walking around yet. I packed a ham and cheese sandwich and some peanut butter cracker things the girls take with them to school. I think I have enough time to write about what happened.

After work that night, two Fridays ago, I stopped at the liquor store on my way home. I bought a two-liter of Coke and a fifth of Jack Daniels. As I walked out of the store a guy bumped into me and mumbled something. "Excuse me," probably. I saw the handle of a gun sticking out of his waistband. I sat in my pickup, a Ford F-150, and watched the man rob the place.

The shrink said details are important. I didn't notice much but the handle of the gun. The woman behind the counter was crying, I could tell even though it was dark. I think she may have wiped her face with her sleeve. She stuffed all the cash from the register into a shopping bag and the man stuck it in his jacket with his free hand. He kept the gun pointed at the woman until he passed through the door.

I didn't think.

When he passed my truck he was barely starting to jog. I opened the door and ran after him. I didn't close the door behind me, just ran. The guy heard me and I think he looked back. He was running now. His gun was in his pocket and I watched it bounce with each of his strides. The liquor store is in a strip mall, almost perfectly in the middle. I counted when I was in my truck. Six stores on the left of it and seven on the right. We were running on the longer side. I was on his heels by the last store.

I dove and tackled the guy on the cold cement. He pushed the palm of his hand into my face. It smelled like an ashtray. I swung my fist and hit him in the chest. Or shoulder. I pulled on his arm and got his hand out of my eyes, the odor stuck in my nose. I could feel his other arm under my knee, wrestling for the gun in his pocket. I swung hard and caught him in the jaw. I shoved my hand into his pocket and gripped the gun. I jerked it out and threw it across the empty parking lot toward my truck.

I remember the metallic tang of his blood. It was warm on my knuckles. I remember that, too. He was still pushing on my face and struggling beneath me. I swung with both fists. I heard his nose break, felt the skin melt under my knuckles. I wanted to knock him out. So that I could tie him up or call the cops.

I heard a voice then, and, for a second, thought it was God. No shit. But when I looked up from the man's swelling face it was the woman from the liquor store. She was still crying. Or crying again. I pressed my knees into the man's chest. I couldn't tell what the woman was saying, but she was waving a phone in one hand, so I figured she had called the police.

I swung again. My fist making contact, his jaw cracking. The shrink called it a convergence. Two things coming together, meeting at a single point.

The guy wasn't moving much anymore. His face was covered in blood and his eye had already swollen enough that he couldn't open it. The woman from the liquor store stood there staring. Then I saw lights from the police cars.

x x x

The company shrink gave me this little notebook. He said it would be a good idea. A way to express what's been going on in my head. I don't really know where to start. Am I telling a story? To who? The shrink didn't tell me that.

My name is Sam. Sammy to my friends. I'm a driver for UPS. "What can brown do for you?" and all that. A shop owner on my route once said our slogan to me as I was carrying a box through the front door. "Yeah, we're big on brown," I said. Later I felt like an idiot. The guy was a native. Tlingit, or something, and I worried he took it wrong. I've always felt funny delivering there since.

It's fall and the leaves are turning. It's 12:59. My little girls are just heading in from recess. My twins, Elizabeth and Cadence. My wife, Olivia named them. I'm not eating much on account of writing too much.

But I don't want to do it at home, last thing I need is to hear how I'm not paying enough attention to my wife. But the shrink was right, there's something addictive about this.

This time I'm in the parking lot of a doctor's office. I just made my last pick up of the day. The receptionist pointed at my picture in the newspaper and shook my hand. She called me a hero and I felt nauseated. How can I write about what happened? Everything is still a blur. I've only slept a few hours in the days since. I lie in bed with my eyes open all night. My wife snores. I didn't know that before.

I need to drive back to the processing center, go home for the night. It's 7:05.

x x x

I had my last fifty-two deliveries done by 1:30. I'm back in the park. I had pick-ups at a toy store and a real estate company.

When the police came they handcuffed the man and shoved him into the backseat of the squad car. "Shit, you did a number on him," one of the officers said. I gave them my statement and they told me I'd need to come to the courthouse the next day for the injunction. I nodded through everything. They had found the gun almost all the way back by the front tires of my truck.

"It'll have my prints on it," I said. "I had to get it out of his pocket."

One officer said, "We need more people like you." The other said, "There's a thin line between brave and stupid."

I couldn't stop shaking all night. "What would the kids and I have done if something happened to you?" Olivia said. I told her what both the cops said. "You're brave and stupid," she said and fell asleep with her hand laying across my chest. Not even that made me feel at ease.

x x x

It's 7:45. I'm headed home. Well, about to head home. I just remembered how the woman from the liquor store ran up and kicked the guy in the gut after I stood up.

"Bastard," she said and it was so loud echoes ping-ponged around the strip mall. It reminded me of high school, getting my ass kicked behind the gym by a couple of seniors from the basketball team.

x x x

It's 2:05 a.m. I couldn't stay in bed any longer. I'm sitting in the living room with the TV on. I put it on mute so it won't wake anybody. My wife was snoring again. The first time I heard her do that a few nights ago I laughed and thought I was going to wake her up.

It's funny when you've known someone so long, but still don't know little things about them. This is what the shrink was talking about, I think. That this whole thing got me so rattled because I didn't know what I was capable of in that kind of situation.

All I see when I close my eyes are bruised skin and blood. Maybe the doctor was right. I hadn't been in a fight since that time in high school.

I need to sleep.

x x x

I'm sitting in my truck again. I'm always in my truck. But this time I'm on the side of the freeway, outside Anchorage. I'm only five miles off my route, but I'm heading in the wrong direction. I should be going north.

I'm not really talking myself out of anything. I thought about driving to the jail, trying to visit the guy and apologize for beating him up.

"You shouldn't be robbing liquor stores," I want to tell him, but he probably already knows that.

x x x

I stopped at a little diner in Girdwood. It's 11:58. A hundred eighty-six deliveries not made, not to mention pick-ups. I turned off the radio in the truck, dispatch must be having fits.

x x x

I drove to Portage Glacier. The ice, what's left of it, is gray. Small waves are cresting white between the ice and when I watch them closely enough I see them swirl in and out of each other. It's 1:42. I'm sitting in a parking lot outside a little ski town, staring at a disappearing glacier.

My cell phone was ringing for twenty minutes straight before I picked it up. It was Olivia.

"They're freaking out at the office," she said. "Where are you? Why isn't your radio on?"

"I'm not on my route," I said. "Don't worry, I'll be back in a few hours." I snapped the phone shut.

My phone is ringing again. Probably Davidson, my supervisor.

x x x

It wasn't Davidson, it was the shrink calling from Davidson's phone. I could hear Davidson in the background, though.

"Tell him he's going on mental health leave," he said.

"There are a lot of people who love you," the shrink said and I told him I knew that. "A lot of people would miss you."

"What do you think I'm doing?" I asked.

"Think about your daughters," he said. "It's not easy growing up without a father."

"I'm not killing myself," I said. "You told me to take time to myself, to think." I told him to tell Davidson I'd have the truck back by the normal time, that I was sorry for missing all the deliveries.

"Mental health leave," Davidson said.

I hung up.

x x x

It's 4:12. I'm back in my truck using a spare shirt to dry my hair. I laid on my back in the parking lot. I leaned back and watched the water flow between the ice. I closed my eyes. The first wave barely reached my hair. The second one didn't even come close, except a few splashes that felt more like rain. The third wave crashed over my face, slapped me with cold. The tide pulled on me, I practically felt the strain in my neck, trying to take my head back to the sea. I thought about the convergence of contact.

I turned the key in the ignition, but I'm still sitting here. It's getting dark and it'll be a couple hours until I'm back at the garage and Davidson's saying "mental health leave" to my face, his face beet-red like it gets. The guy who robbed the liquor store is still sitting in a cell, where he should be. He probably can't even open that eye yet.

If I could tell him something right now I would tell him, "I never saw it coming."

WHERE WE GO
FROM HERE

Susan watched the male polar bear, tragically named Binky, amble from the small pool at the front of the yard to the half-dome cave at the back made of fake plastic rocks like it was a movie set rather than a zoo. And you'd think in Anchorage, a few hundred miles from the Arctic Circle they could do a little better.

Binky's belly swayed, the fur moving like a great shaggy blanket. Like that character on Sesame Street, the one Jason had, in his clipped speech, called 'Nuffy.

That was when Jason had been a regular two year old who darted in and out of rooms around the house while Susan tried frantically to finish a load of laundry. A two year old who scaled tables, desks, TV stands, and bookshelves like he was just warming up for Mount

McKinley. Before he was a two year old withering in a hospital bed. Before he'd stopped using words altogether.

Susan finished her tall vanilla latte, brushed off the coffee grounds that peppered her tongue, and wiped her finger on her jeans. Her phone buzzed with a text message: Everything OK?

The female polar bear, Trinket, was in the pool, right near the glass now. Trinket looked up and made eye contact. Susan remembered reading in the paper a few years ago that the bears had a cub, that it was sold to a zoo in Asia somewhere. Trinket dunked her head under the water. Susan thought of the countless times she'd hovered over the sink, at home and in the hospital, cupped water in her hands and splashed her face. Waiting to feel refreshed, waiting to feel anything.

She'd promised Raymond she would be back by 2:00 and now it was 2:30. She stood, touched her hand to the glass as Trinket's head bobbed back to the surface.

Jason had been potty training. He was on the young end of the spectrum, but excited about wearing big-boy underwear like his dad. Raymond often spent weekend mornings walking around the house in his briefs, which

Susan had taught Jason to call "tighty whities." They had laughed at his mispronunciations, his d's for t's.

For the first few days at the hospital Jason still insisted on sitting on the toilet. The various drugs they had him on made his pee come out in the spurts of a geriatric prostate. Trinket squatted at the back of the habitat and her posture reminded Susan of the way Jason hunched over himself on his potty seat, curious about what was happening in the toilet below him.

Now Binky was in the water and Trinket was in the shade next to a fraying tractor tire. Susan ate a donut hole from the box she had bought at a gas station between the hospital and zoo. What she really wanted was a cigarette, but they didn't allow smoking at the zoo. At least not so close to the animals, and Susan didn't feel like standing in a designated area on some patch of grass next to a set of trash cans.

Binky floated, his buoyant body suspended just below the surface of the water, concentric ripples moving rhythmically away from his body, his fur undulating like white kelp. Susan was nauseous and a headache pulsed in her temples. The worse Jason's condition got, the less she wanted to be at the hospital.

The less she could be there. Because she did want to be there. More than anything she wanted to be there.

And that Raymond was so damn good, always by Jason's side eating meals, reading newspapers, doing work on a fucking laptop all at the edge of the hospital bed, made Susan feel worse. Half the time he didn't even take his full hour away from the hospital they had granted one another. And he never said a thing when Susan's hour stretched into two. They barely talked anymore, aside from the text messages he sent and she didn't know how to answer.

"How could you let them?" Susan said. "How could you stand it?"

Binky flapped one of his plate-sized paws in the water and rolled onto his side. Susan ate another donut hole. There was one left, and some crumbs.

x x x

On their first night back at home together the house felt emptier than it had when Susan had slept there alone, Raymond staying at the hospital, sleeping on the window seat. Susan hadn't made the bed, and she couldn't remember the last time she'd washed the sheets. There was still a piece of Jason there, in the middle of the bed, where she and Raymond would tickle him. His smell was still there, "new baby" smell, Raymond used to call it, and his laugh.

Raymond walked past, his small bathroom bag he'd kept at the hospital in his hand. They had to reinvent the routines, like the carefully choreographed teeth brushing over the single sink in the master bathroom.

The lock clicked and Susan heard Raymond's electric toothbrush whirr. Instead of undressing, changing into a nighty or pajama pants and a tank top, Susan left on her jeans and sweatshirt. She slid under the blanket and switched off the bedside lamp. She curled onto her side and held her hand between her and Raymond's pillows, where Jason would have lain.

When Raymond opened the door he stood there for a moment. Susan turned her head to see him, a silhouette against the light from the bathroom. The way his gut shifted reminded her of Binky. She couldn't help the connection, or that it made her smile a little (which made her thankful she had turned off the light). There was a happy comfort in his shape, and she couldn't remember the last time she'd felt herself go flush this way.

She watched her husband pull off his jeans by the bathroom's light and change into his pajama pants. When he shut off the light and padded toward the bed, she caught herself holding her breath.

Raymond settled in facing away from Susan, but she scooted against his back. She wrapped her arm around him and he clasped her hand against his chest. She kissed the back of his neck, slid her hand out from under his and down to the waistband of his pajamas.

"What are you doing?"

Susan stopped moving her hand.

"Just going with it," she said, feeling stupid as soon as she heard the words. "Nevermind." She shifted back to her pillow, stared up into the dark.

x x x

"Where do we go from here?" Susan asks Trinket, who is lying by the glass.

Binky is a few feet away, at the pool's edge, swatting a half-deflated basketball. Trinket lifts her head, her yellow-white fur catching bits of sunlight breaking through the snow-heavy September clouds.

Susan puts her hand to the glass, expecting, for one innocent second, Trinket will mimic her action. The bear does not. Trinket lays her head back down and Binky lumbers over, nudges her with a paw. Trinket rolls onto her back. Another nudge, playful and lazy. The way it ought to be, Susan thinks.

Raymond was back at work today. Susan should've been, too. She had been on her way at least, but rather than heading downtown she found herself heading the opposite direction, taking New Seward Highway to O'Malley.

Susan wanted Raymond to ask what she had done during her time away from the hospital. She wanted him to get angry and to yell that she should have been there, like him, by their son's side. She wanted him to call her a bad mother. She wanted him to say something. Anything. Anything at all.

Three children run up to the exhibit, their mother in tow. The kids smack their hands on the glass and shout about the bears, how close it is to the glass.

Binky gives Trinket one last swat on the nose and heads to the cave. The mother smiles at Susan who tries to smile back, but working her facial muscles to mimic the woman's smile makes her feel like a stroke victim.

There is a gust of wind and Susan pulls her coat tight. Winter is coming, but what are nine months of dark to her now?

Susan had heard a tour guide say polar bears don't hibernate like other bears, they wander through winter, foraging for whatever sustenance they can find.

ALL THINGS INFINITE

for Jack Driscoll

I drive four hours in my old man's pick-up, his pine coffin rattling in the bed.

I stopped by his place outside of Palmer, now my place, and picked up his boat. It's a two-person dinghy named "Greenberg" after his favorite ballplayer, whose Hall of Fame induction was the first clipping in my dad's scrapbook. The book ranged from articles about baseball to pictures of halibut caught in Homer or Seward. There was never a night as a kid I didn't see him lug that thing out and set it on the dining room table to do some cutting and pasting.

He built the boat when I was in high school. I had stopped showing interest in fishing, hunting, and every other father-son activity he came up with on his R&R's.

But that didn't stop him from spending two whole trips home sawing, sanding, pounding nails. "How about a trip?" he'd said when the paint dried. I told him I had homework, and he suggested the weekend. "Don't have to head back to the slope until Monday."

I grunted and left the room. He was always trying to fill those two weeks of being home, but I was too busy being upset about the eight weeks he was away.

I hitched "Greenberg" to the truck and headed north on AK-1.

When I was real young, five or six, still interested in sitting on his knee for a tall tale, my dad told Viking stories. "Boy-O," he always started, "we come from a long line of Viking warriors. They knew how to live, what it was all about."

As I got older I was confused. According to my grandfather we were of proud Irish heritage. But the word Viking seemed so important to my dad, the way he let it flow from his mouth with church-like reverence. It wasn't until years later that I started to wonder if he knew anything at all about Vikings.

When I got the call that he'd died the first thing I had pictured was him standing in the tool shed, one eyebrow raised, saying, "Don't go burying your old man. Just put me on a boat, set it on fire, and push me out to sea."

An hour into the drive I pull open the back window into the bed and shout as if the two of us might have a conversation for the first time in fifteen years. "Takes you croaking for me to take all that shit you said seriously," I say. His box slides across the Rhino Lining. "You always did like getting your way."

When he got home from the pump stations for R&R, the first day was spent sleeping. After that it was barbecues, fishing trips, playing catch. Every time I asked why he had to go away for so long it was brushed off with another activity. Or worse, him saying, "The Viking man must provide."

"What was it exactly," I say, "got you so damn hooked on Vikings?"

His coffin clanks into the tailgate as I hit a pothole. I haven't driven his truck since high school, and it feels just like it did then. Like he's watching over my shoulder, ready to grab my hand to show me the right way to shift. "Let out that clutch. Up and over. Third gear, come on." It never mattered how many times I told him that mom had already taught me.

I can practically smell his tobacco-breath breathing down my neck. "Where we going?" he would ask.

"Lake Louise."

"All right, a little fishing."

"Not this time, Pops," I say.

Maybe he shuts up because we're not going fishing, or maybe because I stop talking, too, but the rest of the drive is quiet. At the lake I back the truck up to the dock. Lucky for the old man the weather is shit and no one is out. Not even a deranged angler trying to get every dollar out of his license for the season. I unhitch the boat and climb into the truck bed to retrieve the coffin, on its side all the way up by the cab. The weight shifts in the box, and there's a thump of my father's body as I lay it back down.

The last time I saw him my divorce had just been finalized. He came waltzing into my office on the fourth floor of the BP building in Anchorage. "Thought I could take you for a drink," he said. I didn't look up from my computer. "That's right. Work, work, work. No sweat." He pulled a flask from his back pocket and took a long drink, then set it on my desk. "To all things infinite," he said, and with a hint of a wink, "and to some that aren't."

And that, as he liked to say, was that. "You can borrow it," he said, pointing at the flask, still sitting between my keyboard and an empty spot where a framed picture of my ex had sat. Then he walked out the door.

It's not a one-person job, but I lift an end of the coffin and lean it against the boat, then I pick up the other end and shove it between the benches. I take a crowbar and pry open the lid. The old man's face is blue-gray, but his trademark white beard is brighter than fresh snow. His hair had gone completely white at sixteen and he had been famous for it from then on.

I slide his flask into his jacket. "Be seeing you." I lower the lid and use the crowbar to knock back in the nails.

According to my father, Vikings set funeral boats on fire by shooting flaming arrows at them once they were in the water. But I don't have a bow, so I get the boat in the water and douse it with lighter fluid. I try to think of words to say. A eulogy, a limerick, anything. Once, the pump station was shut down because of a category two blizzard. He called home and said it was "just another day in paradise." The same thing he said anytime I asked about work. It didn't matter if they'd been in the thick of a blizzard or digging a trench all day.

"Here's to another day in paradise." I light a match, toss it in the boat as I give the hull a shove with my foot. It parts the water, waves rippling from its prow as flames burst to life.

When my ex and I had tried to salvage our marriage the therapist told me I needed to forgive my father for being gone so much of my childhood. She said he and I needed to reconcile. Catherine had nodded along. "You should drive out and see him," she said. "He's probably lonely."

At the time I hoped she was right. Mostly for trying to make me in his mold. For years he told me when I finished high school he'd get me a job and we would work side by side. Like doing construction was a birthright.

I didn't drive out and see him, though. Not until Catherine decided therapy wasn't working and dropped the divorce papers on the table on her way out of the house. He fixed glasses of iced tea, and we sat on lawn chairs in his front yard. "I ever tell you why I built this house?" he asked and I shook my head. "Your mother told me she was pregnant. I bought the lumber and called some friends. We were living in a shack then. I had gotten the land cheap, but never had the time to build anything permanent." He stopped to look around the yard, sip his tea. "This is going to be yours one day," he said, as if it were a kingdom.

"I have a house," I said. He nodded and we finished our drinks in silence.

The sun is starting to go behind the mountains and the boat has come to a stop maybe twenty yards out. Sparks are crackling in the twilight. The smoke hovers in the air, disappears in the dark. I stare into the flames, where they go pale yellow, imagine I can see him there. I can hear the way he whistled while doing chores around the house. They were always hybrid tunes, mashed up Irish folk songs and Top 40 hits. "Danny Boy" and "Staying Alive," as if there were no division, artistic or generational, between the two.

The two of us dug a fire pit one Saturday morning, then went back to the store for hot dogs and marshmallows. But before dark he got a call that he was needed back on the pipeline. "Jefferson's got a family emergency," he said, already starting to pack.

I go back to the truck, check the cooler he kept in the backseat. There's a lone can of Molson Ice, I pop it and take a long drink. Sitting on the dock I can feel the heat from the flames, think for a second that if I had planned ahead we could have finally had that cookout. "How about that?" I say.

I had agreed on a funeral home the lawyer recommended, and a moderately priced plot at Valley Memorial not far from my dad's house. But I told the mortuary I'd deliver the body myself to save money.

Beads of sweat roll down the sides of my face. I finish the beer, crush the can against the wood beneath me. Orange water shimmers from the reflection of the flames stretching back to the shore. I stand up and hurl the can, landing it a few feet off the side of the boat.

My father had barely made it home for my mother's funeral. He spent the whole time shaking his head, muttering. "This isn't how it should be." But she had planned for her death, bought a plot without him knowing. She had written a will, too. "She kept it behind the cereal," he told me, holding the manila envelope in the static air between us. "All these years and I didn't know."

"Not like you were around to dig in cupboards," I said, the words coming out too quick for me to stop them.

The flames are starting to die. It feels weird to think about leaving, but there's nothing left to be done. "Later," I say, loud enough to reach what's left of the boat, and it echoes around the lake.

The last conversation I'd had with my father started out with me calling to tell him about an eight-hundred-pound halibut caught down in the Peninsula. I wanted to offer to save the article for him, but he invited me fishing and I had to tell him I couldn't. That I was in the middle of a trying to get a big contract finalized.

"Shouldn't work so damn much," he said. "Not healthy."

"At least I'm not spending all my time away from my family."

"What family?"

I took a deep breath. "Sorry I can't go fishing, Dad."

He coughed and it turned into a long sigh. "There's no rule book for fathering, Boy-O," he said. "I did my best and you turned out all right from where I'm sitting."

"What's that mean? I'm not in jail? I work in the oil industry?"

"You were a good kid. Still are."

"Great," I said. "That's why you wanted to be around."

"It was my job."

"You chose your shifts. We all knew it." He didn't say anything more, and I hung up.

I get back in the truck and turn the key. The flames catch my eye in the rearview. I drive back to Palmer and this time it's only the empty boat trailer doing the rattling.

I unlock the front door and walk into the house my dad built. It's the first time I've been home in years, but nothing's changed. Upstairs I slide into my father's bed, pulling the patchwork quilt over me. As I fall asleep I imagine what the headline might be in the paper. I know I'll dig the scrapbook out of my dad's desk in the morning. And I'll clip the article about the Viking funeral at Lake Louise, paste it right on the cover of the damn thing.

Stories in this collection previously appeared in the following publications: "The Long Grass" in *Word Riot*; "The Piñata" in *Pear Noir*; "All Things Infinite" in *The Potomac Review*; "Like Swimming" in Atticus Books Online; "The Pit Bull's Tooth" and "Guilt Names" in *Wigleaf*; "Trench Swimmer" as part of The Next Best Book Club's "Tell Me A Story" feature; "The Run" in *Glasschord*; "The Bathroom Wall" in *The Santa Fe Literary Review*; "WEST" in *PANK*; "Model Home" in *elimae*; "Nothing but the Dead and Dying" in *Keyhole Magazine*; "Mammoth" in *Thumbnail Magazine*; "The Haul Road" in *Corium Magazine*; and "Love and Death in the Moose League" appeared as a stand-alone ebook from Mendicant Bookworks.

ACKNOWLEDGEMENTS

A book six years in the writing is not the work of one person. None of these stories would exist without Craig Lesley, or the other amazing writers I was given a chance to work with during my MFA at Pacific University: Pete Fromm, Jack Driscoll, Bonnie Jo Campbell, and Brady Udall.

Thank you to the editors who published individual stories, and all those who read versions of this manuscript over the years and had encouraging words.

Dawn Marano spent a year whipping these stories into shape with me. From our first conversation she got what I was trying to do and I have infinite appreciation for the care that went into her edits and advice.

To my sons: If you ever read these stories I hope they show you a piece of my home and my heart.

Lastly: Thank you to my wife, Lisa, who has supported my writing from day one and now provides key edits and insights to my manuscripts (and puts up with my moody reception to both). It takes a hell of a human to put up with a writer.

Ryan W. Bradley has pumped gas, changed oil, painted houses, swept the floor of a mechanic's shop, worked on a construction crew in the Arctic Circle, fronted a punk band, and managed an independent children's bookstore. He now works in marketing and designs book covers. He is the author of eight books, including *Code for Failure* and *Winterswim*.

OFFICIAL

CCM ◉

GET OUT OF JAIL
* VOUCHER *

- -

Tear this out.

Skip that social event.

It's okay.

You don't have to go if you don't want to. Pick up
the book you just bought. Open to the first page.

You'll thank us by the third paragraph.

If friends ask why you were a no-show, show them
this voucher.

You'll be fine.

- -

We're coping.

◉

CPSIA information can be obtained
at www.ICGtesting.com
Printed in the USA
FFOW04n1924240316
22609FF